THE
CATSKILL
FAIRIES

By *Virginia W. Johnson*

ILLUSTRATED BY ALFRED FREDERICKS

NEW-YORK HISTORICAL SOCIETY

APPLEWOOD BOOKS ∘ *Publishers of America's Living Past*
CARLISLE, MASSACHUSETTS

THE CATSKILL FAIRIES
was originally published in 1876 by
Harper & Brothers Publishers, New York.

This reprint is reproduced from an
original edition in the collection of
the New-York Historical Society

Thank you for purchasing an Applewood book.
Applewood reprints America's lively classics—books
from the past that are still of interest
to modern readers. For a free copy of
our current catalog, write to:
Applewood Books, Box 27, Carlisle, MA 01741

ISBN 978-1-4290-9802-1

For information about this edition, please write to:
Applewood Books, Box 27, Carlisle, MA 01741.

THE CATSKILL FAIRIES.

CATSKILL FAIRIES.

By VIRGINIA W. JOHNSON,

AUTHOR OF

"JOSEPH THE JEW," "A SACK OF GOLD," "THE CALDERWOOD SECRET," "KETTLE CLUB SERIES," &c., &c.

ILLUSTRATED BY ALFRED FREDERICKS.

NEW YORK:

HARPER & BROTHERS, PUBLISHERS,

FRANKLIN SQUARE.

1876.

CONTENTS.

THE CATSKILL FAIRIES.

ALL ABOUT JOB.

"ARE you afraid to stay alone?" asked Grandfather, drawing the buffalo-robe over his knees, and taking the reins.

"Not a bit afraid," said Job, sturdily, with all a boy's indignation at the charge of cowardice.

"You are twelve years old, and almost a man! Well—take care of the cow, and don't forget the fowls. I shall be back by noon, mebbe."

Then the old wagon creaked away down the hill, moving as if it had rheumatism in all its joints, the white horses jogged off soberly, the rim of Grandfather's hat disappeared, and Job was left alone.

The boy was half afraid all the same. There was not a living soul left on the mountain besides Job, after Grandfather had gone. When one is only twelve years old, and is left in this way, one must feel rather queer at first—at least Job did, and that is all we can know about it. He stood in the road until the last sound of the wagon had died away in silence, and at that moment a little shiver of loneliness crept down his back, and he did not know whether to laugh or cry. Something white and soft brushed against him; it was the Angora cat. You must not suppose that she was an every-day sort of tabby, such as is found in all farm-houses: she was very different from common animals, as we shall presently see. At that moment the cow lowed in her shed, in a friendly way. Job laughed instead of crying.

"He's gone," said the lad aloud. "Now, Kitty, let us have our supper."

He decided to prepare the evening meal just because he did not know what else to do. The cat was placed in a chair, while he spread the board; and as her table manners were very elegant, she merely sat there winking sleepily instead of trying to dab her paws into the dishes.

"This is better than living in the woods—isn't it, puss," said

Job, pouring some milk in a saucer. "How cold you looked that September morning, after the frost, when I found you on the edge of the ravine."

"Miouw!" replied the Angora cat.

"Yes, indeed," continued Job, as he cut a slice of bread for himself. "If you had not come to me, Tom Smithers would have caught you, and carried you down the mountain to all his brothers and sisters—and a nice life they would have led you. The baby would have pulled off your tail the first thing, and how would you have looked without your tail? There! eat your milk."

It really seemed as if the Angora understood every word that Job said, for she gave a little leap in the air, purred violently, and proceeded to eat daintily. After that the cow was made comfortable for the night, the hen-house barred securely, so that no stray fox might steal in, and fresh wood brought from the wood-pile for the fire. There was nothing more to be done before going to bed, and Grandfather as well as Job was usually asleep as soon as the chickens—but then the earliest cock that crowed did not catch them napping in the morning. Before closing the house door, he paused one moment to look at the sky, which was flooded with gold from the setting sun. Job was a very ignorant child, but he knew that far away down the path of shining Hudson River was a great city and the sea. This city he had never seen, which was not very strange, since a great many grown people living back among those Catskill Mountains were equally unlearned. It was the last of December; summer had faded, but the autumn had been long and mild. The mountains towered up blue and grand against the heavens, and it seemed as if the snow would never come from the bleak North this year.   Here and there the hills had a white line on their slopes, as if they had trimmed their robes with ermine, yet the peaks were still uncovered.

Far down in the shadowy hollow was the spot where Rip Van Winkle had slept for twenty years, according to the legend.   All through the leafy Junes, the glowing Octobers, when the woods burned in scarlet and crimson, and the cold, silent winter, Rip must have slumbered.   No wonder he was stiff when he awoke at last.   Job had been to the very spot, and tried to feel sleepy also.   Grandfather said the story was all nonsense, yet somehow Job believed it.   Yes, and far away, over on the brink of a distant precipice, was the hotel, now deserted and gloomy, where the gay people flocked in the warm weather.   Job would hide behind the bushes, like a shy, wild animal, and watch these strangers, wondering much that they cared to gather the wild flowers and mosses which he never noticed. What fun it would be if a bear should come up the path, only all the bears were gone. There was not even a rabbit to be seen. If a pedler should pass, Job would invite him to stay and rest. A pedler's pack was to Job what a dry-goods store is to a city boy.

He went into the house, bolted the door, and crept into bed, where he soon fell fast asleep, with the Angora cat curled up comfortably beside him.

Now we must paint our hero's portrait, because we can feel but little interest in the hero, if, in these days of photography, we do not know exactly how he looked. Job was a strong, active boy, and his face was as brown, his cheeks as red, as the sun and the wind could make them. He wore a battered hat, when he remembered to put it on, and a jacket made of Grand-father's old plum-colored coat, with the tails cut off: Grand-father being a tailor after his own fashion. When spring came he tossed his heavy shoes into a cupboard, and ran about bare-footed, until the frost compelled him to seek them once more.

He had been sent to the little red school-house three miles away, where he learned to read and write. Nobody knows what strange fancies came into his head about the clouds and the moon, living up there alone with Grandfather. This may seem rather a sad, dreary life to the little men who were born in merry, crowded nurseries, yet it is astonishing how much Job found to amuse him. Indeed, he seldom played with other children, and did not miss them.

There was the early breakfast to get, and the dishes to clear away afterwards; then the cow must be driven to the pasture, where the mountain grass made her yield such sweet milk. After that Job could run wild among the rocks all the morning, setting snares for birds, searching for hidden nests, and fishing for trout in the clear brooks, which leaped from stone to stone with gleeful music. Nor did his resources fail him in winter, when the wild storms kept him in-doors. Then he listened to Grandfather's stories about Indians and rattle-snakes, or read the few tattered volumes their library boasted. Better still was it to retreat to the store-room, where their pro-visions were kept as carefully as if they were in a besieged city, and draw figures on the door with a bit of charcoal for a pencil. These crooked, wavy lines meant to the young artist the horses and people of the city.

Grandfather was a bent, wrinkled old man, who smoked a pipe, and grumbled — but he was kind for all that. Job did not take scoldings to heart, for he knew very well that Grand-father was fond of him as the only relative left him in the world. When one lives in a small house alone on a mountain, one has to learn to do everything: Grandfather sewed, made famous bread, and churned the butter. If Job had been used to any other housewife, he must have found it very funny to see Grandfather sweep the rag-carpet with his spectacles on; but to the boy this was the most natural thing in the world.

The mildness of December had tempted Grandfather to make one more visit to the village, for when the storms came they were cut off completely from all intercourse with the val-leys by the deep snow-drifts. He went to buy some food, and to cross the river to Germantown, where a farmer owed him a little money. These dollars must be got, and hidden away in an old pocket-book for the time when Job would be a man. If Job had gone as well, who would have taken care of the cow and the fowls?

Next morning Job was awakened by the Angora cat. Pussy had jumped on his breast, and was licking his cheek with a little red tongue. The fact of the matter was, she had been up a long while, and was becoming very much bored, as well as hungry. Job sprang out of bed, and ran into the kitchen. Something strange had happened! The old clock ticked solemnly in the corner, pointing a hand, as if in reproof, at the hour of ten. Yes, it was ten o'clock, and Job had never slept so late before. The kitchen looked just the same. There was the little table by the window, where Grandfather's large Bible lay, and the shelf above, with the conch-shell on it. The fire was out, and it was dreadfully cold. Job pulled aside the curtain, and peeped out. All the world had grown white. It was snowing. While he slept the storm had come, filling the ravines, covering the low shrubbery, and crowning the mountains with fleecy masses. Job was not afraid of the snow; he was used to it. He kindled a fire, and both he and the cat warmed themselves. Next he tried to open the house door, and found it already banked up by a drift. Job's face grew very long. How should he reach the cow? There was food and wood enough in the house to keep him alive, but the cow must not starve. The cottage was small and poor, consisting of two rooms, and an attic above. Job ran up-stairs, and looked out of the attic window. He there saw a gray sky, the air misty with falling flakes, and the wide sheet of snow below.

At the back of the house the snow was not equally deep, the building being an obstacle to the growing mass. What do you suppose he did? He went down-stairs again, put on his boots, wrapped his neck in a woollen comforter, took the shovel, and jumped out of the window to make a path to the cow-shed. The poor cow, supposing that she was never to have her breakfast, mooed dismally. Job worked with all his might.

Sometimes the cat sprang on the window-ledge to watch him, but she took very good care not to wet her dainty paws by skipping out-of-doors. At last the path was finished, and Job fed the hungry animal. As he did so he heard the flapping of wings, and the cocks crowed dolefully in the dark hen-house, where they supposed it was still night. He had forgotten them until that moment. Dear me! what was to be done?

Job could not leave the poor biddies to die, when he had seen every one of them come from the egg—wee bundles of down. The hen-house was more difficult to reach than the cow's residence. Job's arms ached, and his feet were cold, yet he took up the shovel valiantly, and began to dig again. What with running to and fro, back to the house to thaw numb fingers at the fire, getting meals, and continuing to make paths, it was late in the afternoon before Job had finished his labors. He was able to throw corn to the chickens only by climbing on a snow-mound, and scattering it through the small window of the hen-house. The fowls did not know what to make of it; they cocked their heads sideways to catch a glimpse of daylight. While at work Job had been quite happy; when it was over he began to feel frightened. The storm was increasing, the wind commenced to moan. Grandfather could not force his way back up the mountain while it lasted, and that Job very well knew. The boy sat down in Grandfather's chair, and burst into tears.

" You are too old to cry," said a grave voice.

Job dried his eyes on his sleeve, and looked up.

" Who are you?" he asked, curiosity conquering fear.

" I am the clock. You should know me by this time."

There it stood in the corner, with a brass ship above the dial that rocked when the pendulum swung.

" I didn't suppose you could talk," laughed Job.

" I usually make enough noise, and I am always on the minute, I hope. I don't mind telling you what you will find out sooner or later—to-night I am bewitched," said the clock, in a rattling way.

The Angora cat yawned, curled her whiskers in a military fashion with both her fore-paws, and added, " Yes, we are bewitched."

" What has bewitched you, I should like to know ?" said Job, now quite at his ease, and wishing to understand matters thoroughly.

" The sea-shell," replied the clock.

Job turned to look at the shell as it lay on the shelf ; it glistened in the dim room like a beautiful pearl. " We are to talk this evening," murmured the shell. " After all, a little boy might spend a more lonely night than here with a clock, a cat, and a shell."

" All great travellers," said the clock, proudly.

" And foreigners by birth," said the cat, whisking her tail. " Besides, I have invited company, and you are to have a present before you go to bed."

" Oh, what is it ?" cried Job, with sparkling eyes. " How can company get here in all the storm when Grandfather can't come ?"

" We shall see," returned Puss, walking to the window, and listening with her ear to the crack.

" We have no legs to carry us about like the cat," sighed the clock, half enviously. " Every one in his place, though."

" The wind brings a message to say that they will be here in an hour," said the cat, returning to the fire. " We must try to amuse ourselves until they come."

" Who are *they* ?" asked Job.

" We shall see," said Puss again. " One can live anywhere, I suppose." This she uttered in a dignified way, as if she were used to much better things, and indeed that was what she desired every one to think. " The Esquimaux dwell in the snow and ice—even their houses are built of snow ; thousands of people crowd together in damp cellars of great cities ; and away off in hot countries the natives would not leave their sandy deserts for any thing. I must be contented here."

" How did you come to know so much ?" inquired the old clock, very impertinently.

" I am a cat of experience," said the Angora in a genteel manner.

Then the clock knew that it had done something amiss, and clattered away, sounding the hour to cover up the blunder ; only it grew embarrassed, and struck full fifteen times, like the silly old clock it was.

" I am sorry to make so much noise, but when I am ready I cannot help it. My little hammer rises up, you know, and will fall again." Having finished this duty, the time-piece was prepared to be more agreeable, and immediately proceeded to tell the following story.

THE OLD CLOCK TELLS A STORY.

"THE first sound you ever heard, Job, was the ticking of my pendulum, and the very first object your baby eyes noticed was my brass ship rocking, always rocking, as it did years before you lived, and has done ever since. Babies are sometimes born out on the ocean and in strange places, but I think that the top of a mountain is a droll place for a cradle. I will tell you all about it. I am really very ancient—quite a grandfather clock, as you may see from my wooden case. I was sent over from London in my youth, and once I was mended here in America by the grandson of the clock-maker who made me. He knew me directly, and said, 'Here is my grandfather's work.' At first I lived in New York, where I was for sale in a shop, until I was bought by a man who had me placed on a sloop to be taken up the Hudson River. It was a long voyage in those days, I promise you, and we were one week on board of the sloop before we reached our destination. Now the great steamboats make the same journey in a few hours. I could tell you the exact time if I were placed on the 'Daniel Drew' in running

order, and not laid on my back with my pendulum tied. However, I have no reason to complain. I was purchased by your
grandfather, Job, to place in the new house where he would
bring his bride.

" Dear, dear ! It seems only yesterday when the newly married couple stepped across the threshold hand in hand. Their
hair was golden, their cheeks like ripe apples, and outside the
door the damask roses bloomed in the sunshine. So long, long
ago, little Job—as you may tell by my worm-eaten case and
rusty works.

" I remember very well that we had unexpected visitors up
here the day before you were born. There had been no living
soul here for years besides the old man : his wife was dead, and
his only daughter gone away. Well, the door stood open, and
I saw a wagon drive up with two women in it. The younger
one rose, and stretched out her hands to Grandfather, who
stood shading his eyes, and looking at her.

" 'Father !' she said, and began to cry.

" 'She would come up the mountain to-day,' said the elder
woman.

" The last speaker was Grandfather's sister, and the younger
one was your mother, Master Job.

" The visitors were made comfortable. The girl promised to
be good, and return to the farm with her aunt next day, after
she had seen her father once more. She had been wilful, and
married a handsome sailor against her parent's wishes. Now
the sailor was wrecked, and she had come all this weary way
across the seas to beg forgiveness.

" The wind blew fresh about the lonely house. I struck

twelve, and before I had ceased the angels had brought you here to live. What do you think of that?"

"It is very funny," said Job. He had never thought of being much smaller than he was then.

"Yes," said the clock. "But when the angels brought you they carried away your mother. You never saw her afterwards. You were a sturdy little fellow, and the aunt did everything for you. She had a goat brought up here, for you to drink the rich milk. The goat behaved very well, although it did not like the quarters much. When the aunt wished to take you away home, Grandfather shook his head. If he was a clumsy nurse, you thrived. Bless you! babies thrive anywhere; and if you don't expect them to live, they are sure to do so.

"You had a wee face—I don't suppose your face will ever be as large as mine — and bright eyes, and you used to sit on the floor with your thumb in your mouth staring at my ship. You never cried much, and soon learned to trot around, climbing as nimbly as a squirrel. So you see the good God sent you as a gift to Grandfather, who lived all alone, and he has toiled for you day and night. I have watched him many a time sitting up long after you were sound asleep to sew your coat or carve a toy. The very least you can do, in return, is to be a good boy, for he is growing old."

Job had never given the matter a moment's reflection. He could not decide whether he had been a good boy or not. Now the old clock's words made a deep impression on his mind, and he formed a resolution.

"He shall never saw all the wood again!" he exclaimed. "Sometimes I forget, you know."

" That is right," said the clock, heartily.

" You will always be glad if you are thoughtful of others," said the sea-shell.

" Grandfather is a good man; he gives me tender morsels," said the Angora cat gratefully.

The old clock had finished its story, and for a few minutes nothing was heard in the room but the slow, steady ticking of the long pendulum as it swung back and forth, and the quiet purring of the Angora cat. Job was thinking of what the clock had told him, when the silence was again broken by the sea-shell.

ADVENTURES OF A SEA-SHELL.

" Each one may tell what he knows," said the sea-shell, in a soft, liquid voice.

" Where did you come from? I mean, where did you grow?" asked Job, eagerly.

A sweet little laugh came gurgling from the depths of the shell as water bubbles out of a clear spring hidden among the moss of the woods.

" Where did I grow? You speak as if I was plucked from the branch of a tree like fruit. Do you not know that a little, soft, defenceless animal — a mollusk — built me for a strong castle to protect it from foes? Then, being something of an artist in its own tiny fashion, the mollusk painted and decorated its house, lining it with pearl, as you see, and adding turrets to the roof. Yes, and the very best of it was that it had only to close the door firmly, and no enemy could come in; even the rough waves might toss the house about with no harm to the inmate."

" Where did you live?" persisted Job.

" I was only the strong castle remember. The mollusk lived away off in the tropical waters of the Indian Ocean. Above the sea bloomed the rich islands where the spice-trees grow, and cruel pirates lurked along the shore to attack foreign vessels. The pirates, in their swift boats, were like the small sword-fish that dart forth to attack the whale, wounding the huge creature on all sides.

"Chinese junks came there, too, in search of the swallow nests, built in the rock caverns, which they sold in their markets for the famous bird-nest soup. Down at the bottom of the ocean crawled the sea-cucumber, a slow creature, with a transparent body, and pretty, feathery tentacles, like plumes, waving about the mouth, to draw in food. Even the cucumber was not safe from the sharp Chinese eyes. Whirr! a prong was hurled through the water, striking the poor thing with unerring aim, and up came the cucumber to the surface, to be packed as the 'trepang' of commerce. If we hide in the deepest waters, we do not escape; nothing is safe from man. I left my home one day, with a sudden jerk, just as the trepang did. The mollusk soon died, out of the sea, even as you would die if your head was held under water. I was left, being only a shell, and since then I have been a great traveller. Your mother brought me here in a box. First I was carried off by a sailor as a gift for his sweetheart at home; yet I never saw the sweetheart, for the cabin-boy stole me long before we reached port. The cabin-boy treated me very ill: he traded me for a gay neck-tie, when I would have really brought him money if sold for a cabinet. Silly fellow! Then we sailed up north; I could tell you all about the cold countries."

" It is cold enough here," yawned the Angora cat.

" I changed owners half-a-dozen times among sailors. We were in the Baltic Sea, and I had been left on deck carelessly, when a gull came swooping down on me, made bold by hunger.

" 'You are as tough as a Tartar,' said the gull, pecking at me to judge if I was good to eat.

" 'What is a Tartar?' I inquired.

" 'Don't be tiresome,' said the gull, pettishly. 'My grandfather knows everything: ask him.' Then it flew away. I was glad to have the ship lurch just then, and roll me against the bulwark out of sight. Presently the gull returned, hopping along cautiously in the hope of stealing a morsel.

" 'Where is your grandfather?' I asked.

" 'Holloa! Are you still there, Mr. Shell?' cried the gull, cocking its head over its shoulder.

" ' I will make a bargain with you,' I said. ' If you carry me to your grandfather, I can tell you where to find food.'

" ' But you are so heavy,' he objected.

" ' But you are so hungry,' I said, quietly.

" ' I know it,' groaned the gull. ' I will try to find the old gentleman instead.'

" Then it flew away again, returning with the grandfather gull, and I kept my word by showing the birds where they could obtain food near the cook's galley. The old gull said he did not know what the young one meant about Tartars, but he would tell me a story, if I would excuse his standing on one leg while speaking, for he had the gout badly in his right claw. He told me the following tale.

HOW BIORN DISCOVERED AMERICA.

" ' THE Northern nations were a roving people long before their existence was known in Southern Europe. The Goths crossed the Baltic Sea in three ships, to grow into a mighty race capable of subduing Rome ; the Swedes were rulers on the ocean, strong in arms and numbers ; the Danes boldly attacked the English coast, and, after being held in check by Alfred the Great, established four Danish princes on the throne. A Scandinavian king ruled in Dublin ; early conquests were made of the Shetland Isles and the Hebrides ; Scotland was visited by them, when Duncan defeated the invaders, the Scots being commanded by Macbeth and Banquo.

" ' The country was too small for all the families to be fed and lodged, so it was agreed that a certain number of children to each household should go abroad in search of a living. There were too many birds in the home nest. The father drove out his sons when they grew to manhood—except the eldest son, who was heir to the estate. The sea-kings, or vikings, spread their sails to discover new lands. Naddod, a Norwegian pirate, saw one day a dreary looking country, which he named Snowland ; then Gardar Svarfarson, a Swede, found that it was an island, and called it Iceland instead, because of its forbidding aspect. His companions liked the island, and a Norwegian Jarl took refuge there, founding a colony.

" ' Then the sea-kings sailed on, and other shores were found in the Western Atlantic. In the year 982 a Jarl of Norway went to Iceland, with his son Eric the Red, and Eric left Iceland to roam still farther to the south-west, where he espied a country which he named Greenland, and made his home at Eric's Fiord. Heriolf, one of these early colonists, was a trader, sailing from place to place in partnership with his son Biorn.

" ' Now we shall hear! Biorn, who was a sort of salt-water pedler, had agreed to meet his father at a certain spot, but missed him on the open ocean. Lo! a terrible gale arose, driving Biorn's vessel like a feather before the wind. The little craft bounded lightly over the heaving billows, through sleet and foam—sent far away from the shelter of Greenland, until the sailors expected that her prow would touch the end of the world. At last they saw land, a wide region, thick-

ly wooded. It was a northern cape of the Gulf of St. Lawrence.

" ' What do you suppose this stupid

Biorn did? He just drifted around the promontory, looked at it, and, without setting foot on the shore, spread his sails before a fresh west wind, the storm having abated, and returned to Greenland, where he found his father Heriolf safely harbored.

"'That is the way Biorn discovered America, quite ignorant that he was the first European to touch the strand of a wonderful New World. This happened long before Christopher Columbus saw the tropical palm-trees and crystal waters of the West Indies. Biorn went back, and told the story at least. Eief, a son of Eric the Red, set sail with thirty-five men, reached the American coast, and steered along it until he found an inviting anchorage. The region was delightful: fruits and berries were ripe, and there was salmon in the river. The Northmen landed, built huts, and called the spot Vinland, because of the quantities of grapes they found. Lief spent a winter in Vinland, then sold his vessel to his brother Thorwald in the spring, who stayed another year, exploring the land. The natives came in canoes to oppose him, and Thorwald was killed. The other Northmen remained a third winter. The natives were like the Esquimaux, already known in Greenland.

"'In 1007 a rich Greenlander, Thorfin, emigrated to Vinland with sixty followers and his wife Gudrida. The ships carried all kinds of animals and food. Gudrida was the first European woman to see the New World, and her son Snorro, born at Vinland, was the first child of foreign parents in America. Thorfin's expedition prospered. The native tribes came in great numbers to trade in furs, yet Thorfin went home again.

" 'At the mouth of the St. Lawrence traces of these early settlers have been found. The savages there were different in aspect, and they knew the cross when the Jesuit missionaries showed it to them.'

" I have told you the truth, whatever else you may hear to-night," concluded the shell.

" So did I tell the truth," said the clock. " I don't know what the cat may do."

" Speak for yourself, then," said Puss, quite in a huff. " I have had no chance to tell my story yet, if you please; and it seems to me that both of you are fond of hearing yourselves talk.—Oh !"

A little mouse had crept out of its hole ; the cat pounced on it like a flash.

" I can't imagine why you like those mice," said the clock. " It makes me tremble in all my wood-work only to see one, they have such frightfully sharp teeth, and gnaw such dreadful holes."

The Angora cat was terribly excited ; her eyes were large, her whiskers bristled, and she held the poor little mouse between her paws. One could see how much she was like those great relations of hers, the tiger and lion, when they gloat over their prey.

" What have you got to say for yourself," growled Kitty.

" Mercy !" squeaked the little mouse, rolling its eyes towards Job.

" Let Mousey go. You have had your supper," said Job.

" Ask me nicely, mouse, and perhaps I will," said the wicked cat, enjoying the fright of her captive.

C

So the little mouse sat on its hind-legs, and crossed its fore-paws piteously.

" I am very young to die. I ran away from the nest behind the beam of the cellar just to see life. Oh! please don't look at me like that!" it said faintly.

" I will not eat you if you tell a story," said Puss.

" Oh, dear!" piped the little mouse. " How can I tell a story? I have no ideas, and I have never been even to a mouse school yet. I am really a baby. To be sure, we have gnawed a great many books and papers; still we do not read the print—we only make nests."

" Do you stay in the corner of the hearth and think of a story," said the cat. " If you try to run away I will eat you in one mouthful. There! I don't mind your being a baby mouse at all; your bones will be all the more tender on that account."

So the little mouse had to sit in the corner, and make the best of it. When the cat looked at it, the mouse closed its eyes, pretending to nap, for it wished to appear very much at ease, but it trembled in every limb for dread of those terrible jaws and gleaming eyes.

It was now the cat's turn to tell a story.

ONE OF A CAT'S LIVES.

" I KNOW very well that I was born in a palace—that is, a palace in comparison with this cottage," said the Angora cat, stretching herself comfortably on the warm hearthstone.

" What was it like ?" asked Job, glancing around the kitchen.

" Well, it must have been a palace, because there was a lawn and a park, with winding avenues and flowers. Then the house was beautiful, large, and spacious, with soft carpets and velvet cushions. The old lady who lived there owned twenty cats, and people said she was crazy on the subject of pets. The cats had an easy life. Each morning a servant bathed the Angora family, combed our fur, and tied a fresh ribbon about our necks. How much we were caressed ! One day I was taken to the drawing-room for some visitors to admire my flossy coat, when I saw an ugly face peering in at the window, and I hid beneath the dress of my mistress. The butler told the beggar to go away. ' I'm hungry,' said the man. Now I had never been hungry in my life. After the visitors left I curled myself up for a nap on the best embroidered cushion. Two dirty hands seized me, the ugly face peered in the window again, and I was hurried away, hidden from sight beneath the beggar's ragged coat. In vain I struggled ; he held me firmly until we had crossed the road behind a hedge, and he took me out to shake me angrily.

" ' You are always fed, if the children do starve,' he muttered, fiercely.

" He did not kill me, though I was half dead with fright by the time he reached the miserable hovel where he lived. The children were hungry, but I was made to rob them of their scanty portion of milk, because I was to be taken to town and sold for my beauty.

" Fortunately some dear, kind ladies bought me, paying the man a good price, and I hope that he took the money to the poor children.

" Wherever the ladies went on their travels, I was carried in a basket, and people were warned not to hurt Kitty. At this strangers smiled, but they were all good to me. We crossed the ocean in a large steamship, and in the summer we came up to these mountains. When parties rambled in the woods I was allowed to go, for there were too many children in the hotel for my comfort. They play strange pranks with the most superior cats. When the ladies had a picnic I was attracted by a bird that hopped near in search of crumbs. I gave chase, the bird flew away, and when the people called me I hid behind a rock. I was tired of being petted, so I decided to become a hunter, searching for my own food in the woods. This served very well until the frost came. Then you found me, Job. I made a great many acquaintances in the woods during my rambles, as you will presently see."

" Crickets and grasshoppers ?" said Job.

" No such thing," replied the Angora cat. " Here they are !"

Job could scarcely believe that he was still in his senses, for in a moment the place was full of Fairies. The wee people came through the keyhole, down the chimney, and forth from the blazing logs of the fire, with a soft rustle of wings and a murmur of tiny voices that sounded like the patter of rain-drops among forest leaves. The boy winked several times to make sure he was awake.

At first these visitors looked all alike : their pinions were spangled like those of a butterfly, and their little forms twinkled and hovered about in restless motion ; but by degrees they settled down like fallen blossoms, some on the hearth, others on the chimney-piece, and two perched on the sea-shell. The little mouse moved an inch to run ; Puss clapped a paw on it. Then the Fairies formed a ring around the animal by joining hands, and danced to their own music. The mouse shivered with terror ; but by degrees it grew brighter, and began to dance also, hopping on one hind-leg, and nodding its head in time to the song. That was a droll sight !

Job now saw that the Fairies on the hearth were very plump and pretty. They wore little petticoats of red rose-leaves, while their caps and aprons were made from the white rose's petals.

" I am Queen Puff, and we come from the Lowlands," said one, nodding to Job. " You must excuse us if we keep on with our work while we pay our visit, because we are busy housewives. Besides, this is Christmas-eve."

With that two of her maidens brought her spinning-wheel to Queen Puff, and then all her court took their knitting. Such a spinning-wheel as that was ! The frame was a rose-thorn, the wheel made of horse-hair, and the distaff wrapped in a tangle of cobweb, which the Queen spun off in fine silk threads.

" What is it for ?" asked Job.

" These threads make children's dreams," replied Puff. " Of course there must be a great supply of dream-thread on Christmas-eve for the children of America alone."

Another group was clustered on the handle of the tongs. These were clad in pale satin.

" We are the Fairies of the Mountain Laurel," they said. " You will find us in June on the overhanging banks, where the ferns and mosses drape the rocks, and the rivulets flow down hill. Then we live in our lovely pink houses ; but when our flowers fade we hide beneath the leaves."

" I know you right well, and how glad I am to see you in the spring," said Job.

On the window-sill, where Jack Frost had made the panes like ground glass, a number of delicate forms rested, their robes of snow-flakes, and their helmets of gleaming ice.

" We are the Winter Fairies, and dare not approach the fire," they murmured. " We live in marble palaces made by our king, and there are no jewels so splendid as the icicles with which we hang our halls."

" We are the Summer Fairies," said a race that had sprung from the burning log. They were so radiant that one could not look at them long ; they changed in hue from emerald green to red and purple, and the flame shone through them. The Summer Fairies were as unlike Queen Puff's court as possible, for their faces were brown, their hair dark like the Indians'.

" Where is the Fairy of the Waterfall ?" inquired the cat. " She was to bring Job's gift."

"Winter has made her a prisoner; but she will beg leave to come, if the king is in a good-humor. Sometimes he melts."

"These are friends I made in the woods last summer," said the Angora, proudly.

Just then a queer little form dashed down the chimney, upset Queen Puff's spinning-wheel, and flew into the cat's face as a beetle blunders into the candle-flame.

"Gracious! I hope that I'm not late," said the new-comer.

"Where are your manners?" cried Queen Puff, putting her cap straight.

"Beg your pardon, ma'am. I was in a hurry to see Job."

Then he winked at our hero, and began to laugh. This was Fairy Nip from the Berkshire Hills across the river, and his garments were made entirely of pumpkin-blossom cloth. He carried on his back a pack—for he was a fairy pedler—which he unstrapped and opened.

" Perhaps I may have something to please you, ladies. Here is the latest thing in jackets—fly-wings trimmed with dandelion down ; the effect is quite as good as real lace. My jewelry is cheap ; this set of spider's eggs, necklace, bracelet, and ear-drops, I will sell for a mere song. Want any patent medicines ? Try the Mountain-dew Tonic to make lazy people work, or the Strawberry-seed Cordial for the appetite. As to cosmetics, I can make the plainest fairy beautiful in five seconds by using this Bee Powder."

The Fairies were very much excited ; they crowded around the tiny pedler, who sold his wares like wildfire. Queen Puff left her spinning-wheel, and the Winter Fairies ran great risk of melting because they *must* peep at the pretty things. The Summer Fairies showed the greatest fondness for finery, as they were Indians. They bought mantles of scarlet poppy, and strutted about to be admired ; while of the spider-egg chains they could not get enough.

When Nip had emptied his pack, he cut a caper, winked again at Job, and climbed on the mouse's back, which was a soft, velvet couch. The mouse looked like an elephant to Nip.

The Sprite of the Mountain Laurel began to speak :

" There are fairies in the New World just as much as in the Old, and it is time we should be known. Surely nature has given us quite as beautiful homes as those of our sisters across the seas; we can hold revels in the heart of forests where man seldom comes; we may wrap ourselves in the rainbow mist of the waterfall; and if we wish to live in water mansions, there are plenty of majestic rivers. What sprite could desire a more beautiful home than our dear Hudson yonder? People are stupid, and will not see us."

" They are too busy, I guess," said Nip. " Many a time a farmer has all but crushed me beneath his foot in my beautiful yellow coat, or I have peeped out of a flower-cup under the very nose of a man who was too busy thinking about money-making to see either the flower or Nip. These are the sort of people who tell the world that there are no fairies."

The Laurel Queen said she had a story to tell.

THE OAK-TREE SPRITE.

"At the foot of these mountains an oak-tree once waved its long branches, and towered above the grass bank which sloped away to the brink of a little brook. The brook sang sweet songs to itself all day long, as it rippled about large rocks, then flowed smoothly among rushes and marsh flowers. The birds trilled delicious music overhead; but the oak-tree had no ear for music, although it had lived beside the brook for years, and might certainly have learned something from association by this time.

"'The summer breeze rustles among my leaves, and the winter storms clash my branches together,' said the tree. 'Is not that enough noise?'

"'That amounts to just nothing at all,' replied the brook, the sunshine dimpling its surface with golden sparkles as it hurried on to swell the broad Hudson, and roll still further onward to the sea.

"At last something happened. A lamp burned all night in the poor cottage; the Doctor came with his medicine-box, and the parents hovered anxiously about the cradle. When morning dawned the house had grown still, for in the early hours, before the sun brought returning warmth and brightness to the glad earth, a little soul had risen on snowy wings to the gates of heaven—the child was dead.

" Then the father made a tiny grave beneath the oak-tree's shade, and flowers soon bloomed, tended by loving, careful hands.

" One morning a tall poppy shot up, the petals unfolded, and from this little red house out stepped a sprite dressed in the oak-tree's livery of green. You might easily have mistaken him for a grasshopper or a locust at a short distance. In his hand he carried a carpet-bag, stitched together neatly out of bits of oak-leaf, and on his head he wore the small end of an acorn, fashioned into a cap. Altogether the sprite had a very brisk manner, and as he came out of the poppy mansion he gave it a kick, very ungratefully.

" ' I am just born, and I belong to you,' he said, making a low bow to the oak-tree.

" The tree was delighted with the little man.

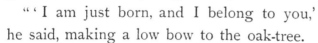

" ' Shelter yourself in my trunk from the cold, and dance among my leaves,' it said, cordially.

" ' What am I to do for you in return ?' asked the sprite.

" ' You will be my voice,' replied the tree. ' The birds shall teach you to sing.'

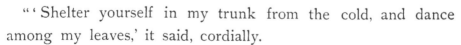

" ' Capital !' laughed the sprite. ' I will hang up my carpet-bag in a safe corner; I must take good care of that, whatever happens.'

" ' Why ?' inquired the oak-tree, much interested.

" ' Because it is a fairy gift.'

" ' A fairy carpet-bag—eh ?' and the tree chuckled.

" The sprite was charmed with the fresh, beautiful world into which he had been born. He roamed all over the great oak-tree, which was a long distance for him to travel, and he was never lonely, as he found no end of delightful society. There were the ants and spiders to chat with about their own affairs, and the stupid caterpillars to poke, for the sprite loved his pranks as well as older children.

" The oak-tree had very sensible ideas about education ; the sprite must not play all the while.

" Soon the news spread that the oak-tree wished to have its sprite instructed, and all the creatures came flocking to discuss the matter, as the tree was a general favorite.

" ' I can teach the sprite to growl,' said the black bear.

" ' Thanks !' said the tree. ' He is such a tiny fellow it does not seem necessary that he should do anything besides laugh.'

" ' I can teach him to burrow in the ground, or to steal chickens,' said a little fox.

" ' I can teach him to swim,' croaked a frog.

" ' And I to dive below the surface,' added a water-rat.

" Now came the beautiful birds, fluttering in a bright cloud to perch on the branches, ruffling their soft feathers, cocking their pretty heads about as they hopped jauntily from twig to twig. The sprite stroked the birds with his little hands, and they chirped gayly.

" ' The oak-tree has sheltered us so often that we will gladly render a service,' said a swallow.

" ' Dear little birds ! teach me to sing,' begged the sprite.

" ' Yes, certainly,' replied a robin. ' We must begin at once, and give you some notes to practice while we are off hunting our breakfast. Listen to me — tra-la-la !'

" The other birds set up a clamor before the sprite could repeat the notes which had swelled pure and sweet from the robin's tiny throat.

" ' The robin is no singer,' piped a saucy wren.

" ' I will show you the way to use your chest notes,' said the thrush.

" ' Bob-o-link ! bob-o-link !'

" ' Peet-tweet !'

" ' Chip, chip, chee !'

" ' The loudest voice is the best,' screamed a handsome crow. ' Caw ! caw !'

" The oak-tree plainly saw that the sprite would be unable to make anything out of all this noise, so it shook its trunk so violently that the birds had to take wing, or tumble to the ground.

" ' One at a time, if you please,' said the tree, politely. ' The sprite is so young that he is easily confused.'

" Then each bird hopped out and sang a song.

" ' All the songs are so sweet that I like one as well as the other,' said the wise and prudent sprite.

" The birds were offended — each wished to have its song preferred to that of the rest ; so they all flew away as suddenly as they came, leaving the sprite to repeat, ' Caw, caw, peet-tweet, bob-o-link,' quite out of tune, because his head was giddy after the lesson.

" One day the sprite noticed a different music. There had

been a storm, and the brook, swollen by mountain torrents, rushed along noisily, instead of rippling calmly, and the break of the waters seemed to the sprite the finest melody he had ever heard. Day by day he listened as the flood gradually subsided, and quietly sang to himself as the brook sang.

" This delighted the oak-tree beyond measure.

" ' Now we have music in ourselves,' said the tree, joyously. ' We shall always be happy.'

" The tree spoke too soon. Ever since its roots had struck into the soil it had stood there on the bank, and it naturally supposed that matters would never be changed.

" Dull blows were heard, and many stately trees toppled over to the ground.

" ' What is it ?' said the sprite, pausing in his play.

" ' The wood-cutters,' said the oak-tree, trembling with fear. ' You will have no home, little sprite, if they fell me.'

" The sprite ran quickly, and hung his magic carpet-bag around his neck. Soon a party of wood-cutters approached, with their sharp axes over their shoulders, and they paused before our oak-tree because it was the finest they had seen. They girdled the brave trunk, and then began their work, each stroke of the cruel steel cutting deeper into the heart of the wood, as well as the heart of the sprite, who wept as he clung to the branch from which he must soon be torn. A shudder of all the leaves, a slow rocking from side to side, and the oak sank down upon the green bank never to rise again.

" The sprite, with his bag about his neck, which made him invisible, sorrowfully watched the men at their labor, while they stripped the boughs, and cut the trunk into logs, so that there

was nothing left but a pile of wood. When they moved these logs, the sprite took his carpet-bag in his hand and trudged after. He decided never to leave his dear tree while a stick of it remained. One of the wood-cutters saw the little man, who was visible when he took his bag in his hand like a traveller.

" ' Halloo ! is that a grasshopper ?' cried the man.

" Instantly the sprite jumped into the grass, and hung the bag around his neck again. From the lumber-yard to the mill, where sharp saws smoothed and polished the logs, did the sprite follow the tree, and at last they reached the shore, where the firm, stout oak was to build a ship. The sprite saw a great deal of the world in those busy places, and learned more than the brook or the birds could ever have taught him.

" ' I was only a baby then,' he thought. ' Now I must be grown up.'

" He roamed everywhere while the ship was building, with the magic bag to protect him. He crept into the old fruit-vender's pocket and spilled her snuff; he peeped into the tin pails which the children brought for their fathers at noon ; and he clambered about the workmen whose hammers kept time on the ship's sides—rat-a-tat-tat.

At last the vessel was finished, and the people gathered to see her launched. The sprite was on board before any one else, however, and perched on the bow when the ship slid gracefully down into the water. There was nothing for the sprite but to become a sailor, now that the dear oak-tree was prepared to follow the sea. He enjoyed himself beyond meas-ure, and he was soon at home in every nook except the medi-

cine-chest. Down in the hold he met the rats, and they were sharp fellows enough.

" ' Ha, ha !' laughed the rats. ' We like new ships, too, so we just skipped on board when all was ready.'

"Some of the rats had already made voyages, and these called themselves 'Jolly Tars,' and other funny names. They told the sprite what to do in case of shipwreck; nor did their good services end in mere empty advice, for they brought him any dainty in the ship's stores which their sharp noses could be poked into, and thus he fared very well.

"When tired of the rat company he went to the captain's cabin, where a lamp swung all night, and the table had its legs chained to the floor, to keep it from running away in rough weather. Here he found a respectable old cat, that told him there were no rats on board, as it was a new ship, therefore she need do nothing but doze on a rug all day. The sprite laughed in his sleeve, for the cat was so old that her whiskers were gray, and she disliked springing about after the nimble rats.

"The captain was a kind-hearted man, and never inflicted suffering on his crew. The mate was harsh and stern, using the rope's-end or his heavy boot, whenever the captain was out of sight, to vent his ill-humor. The sprite tormented the wicked mate, and the rats helped him. The sprite stuck pins into him, pulled his hair, tweaked his nose, tripped him up on the deck, and tied him in the chair with fine threads, until the mate feared that he was bewitched.

"The little cabin-boy was homesick. He had run away, without the consent of his parents, because he fancied that he should like the sea. Now he discovered how sadly mistaken he had been. He must work hard and receive many blows from the surly mate.

"Our sprite pitied the cabin-boy, and when he slept at night in the close forecastle, the elf took off the top of the little lad's

D

head, as you would raise the lid of a tea-pot, and wove dream-pictures in the sleeper's brain.   Then the sprite, after stocking thought with bright-colored ideas enough to last through the next day, just closed the lid of the boy's head, and marched off about other business.   By this means the cabin-boy grew happy, and whistled as he worked.

" The ship sailed on, miles and miles, into warm latitudes, where the soft breeze grew fragrant with the breath of flowers, and the sea gleamed rosy and green at night like sparkling showers of diamonds.   Land could be seen in the distance, looming like a faint cloud on the horizon.

" ' What a beautiful world!' said the sprite, climbing the rigging to admire the clear sky and tranquil water.   ' That is the shore over yonder, and soon we shall see strange roofs and towers, the narrow streets built to shade the people from a hot sun.   The rats told me, and they know.'

" The sprite was not as near the curious towns as he thought, for soon he noticed a cloud rising rapidly, and spreading dark masses over the whole heavens.   The sprite scampered down from the rigging as the tempest came rushing along, heaping up the waves into mountains, and washing over the deck.   The surly mate was hurled from the bulwark far out into the heaving waters, and no one heard his death-cry, while the ship plunged and swayed helplessly from side to side.

" The sprite was terrified ; he cowered down in the hold, and the rats nestled close to him, for they had lost their fine spirits, too.   Suddenly a grinding crash announced that the vessel had struck on a reef, and was at the mercy of the breakers.

" ' Every one for himself,' cried the sprite, catching a splinter of wood for a float, and throwing himself overboard. This was what the rats advised in case of wreck, but not one of them succeeded in reaching shore. The waves bore our hero along safely—he was as light as a feather on his oak float; and finally he was tossed up on the shore more dead than alive, as a shipwrecked mariner always is, whether sprite or mortal.

" When the sun rose next morning the brave ship was gone, and all the crew had perished. A little sprite and a bit of wood alone remained.

" ' Ah, if we were only rooted in our home beside the brook,' sighed the bit of wood.

" ' Are you my tree ?' cried the sprite.

" ' Yes ; I have brought you to land, and now you must give me a decent burial on this foreign shore,' said the last splinter of the once grand tree.

" So the sprite found a spot high above the waves, and commenced to dig a grave with his tiny hands; but he got along very slowly.

" ' I have no patience with such clumsiness !' said a Mother Carey's chicken that happened to be strolling past. Then the bird would have helped to make the grave by scraping the sand with its claws.

" ' No, no !' cried the sprite. ' I must bury my own tree alone.'

" The bit of wood was dragged to the hole, and a pebble placed as a head-stone to mark the spot.

" ' The oak-tree is dead,' sobbed the sprite over the grave.

" ' That can't be helped,' said Mother Carey's chicken, pecking at the carpet-bag, which the sprite had laid out to dry.
The sprite put it around his neck, and disappeared before the
bird's round eyes; then appeared again, laughing; until Mother
Carey's chicken did not know what to make of it all.   They
got along well together, however, as the sprite had a cosy way
which won friends.

" ' What part of the world is this?' he inquired.

" ' World?   If you ask such hard questions I must take you
to the mussels.   They know all sorts of things, which are
brought them by the tide.   I have no time for such nonsense,
as I have my living to get.'

" They went to the mussels on a steep cliff jutting out into
the sea, where the waves were running so high that when the
mussels opened their mouths to answer the sprite they only
seemed to gurgle instead of speak.

" ' What do they say?' asked the sprite.

" ' They say that you are a great way from your home,' replied the bird, as he could understand the mussel language
much better than the sprite could.

" The friendly chicken brought the sprite all sorts of things to eat, such as made his own supper, but the delicate stranger could not touch the food.

" ' I will call on you in the morning again.' With that the bird flew away.

" The last prank the sprite ever played was to try on the magic carpet-bag before the amazed Petrel. When the bird returned at sunrise, an oak-leaf lay on the grave of the tree, and the sprite had faded from life."

When the Laurel Queen ceased speaking, some of her fairy audience clapped their hands politely.

" Poor little sprite," said Job.

" I knew the oak-tree well," said a Winter Fairy. " How many times we hung its branches with icicles. It was years ago, to be sure—but fairies never grow old ; the children who believe in us become men and women, and forget us. We are always the same."

" Will somebody please make Nip behave ?" asked the clock, in an injured tone. " I know that he is trying to make mischief with my works by the way he spies through the keyhole of my case. If he pokes me I shall run down, or come to a dead-lock in my machinery, and that has never yet happened to me."

Nip, who had been capering around the kitchen while the Laurel Queen told her story, now assumed the most innocent look.

" Dear me, how touchy you are, Clock ! I was only trying to see how you were made. Perhaps I shall invent a time-piece myself one of these fine days.   It's not uncommon where I come from," he said.

"If you don't go away I shall strike, and that will put me out of order.   Be off with you!" said the clock.

"Come here, Nip," coaxed Job, holding out his hand.   So Nip flew up and sat in the palm of Job's hand, crossing his legs like a Turk.   If Job closed his fingers gently over the saucy elf, he seemed to hold a velvet insect.

The little mouse still crouched in the corner, not daring to say its body was its own while the Angora cat's eye was fixed on it.

"It is my turn to tell a story," said one of the Summer Fairies, walking up and down the hearth, wrapped in the red poppy cloak.

RAPP, THE GNOME KING.

" MANY years ago, before the white race came to live on the banks of our Hudson, a certain Elf King decided to give a tea-party on one of these very mountains, and to invite a great prince. He chose a peak over yonder. Do you see the high hill on the right now covered with snow? Well, there the Elf gave his banquet.

" Now the guest was no less a person than Rapp, King of the Gnomes ; and if you never heard of him before, it is quite time he was made known to you. In the first place, he was a dwarf, with green eyes, a red nose, yellow hair of spun gold, and a face of copper. His kingdom was in the depths of the earth ; sometimes he lived in the Rocky Mountains, and again in the Andes. He did not mind stepping from one continent to the other in the least. The volcanic fires such as burst forth from the summits of Vesuvius and Etna were fed by his subjects, and his domain extended over the rocks which are richly veined with gold and silver.

" When Rapp felt ill-humored he liked to bury himself in some remote cavern, and the earth then rumbled with his anger ; but he also enjoyed appearing in the upper world oc-casionally, to see what every one was about. He graciously accepted the Elf's invitation to tea. The clever Elf people had been very busy with the mountain-peak to make it elegant for that day. They smoothed the rough, sharply pointed rocks into slender pillars draped in vines ; a fountain gushed in sparkling jets of spray, and a carpet of velvet moss sloped from the brink of the fountain, fit for the dainty feet about to trip over it. A grotto of pure crystal reflected the light in a thousand glittering pendants, so that it resembled transparent ice. In this grotto was spread a feast of delicious fruits—golden oranges, ruddy apples and pears in silver vases, crimson peaches, and pyramids of amber honey.

" ' I hope everything is in order,' said the Elf King. He was very small, but he wore a red smoking-cap on his head, and slippers on his feet, crochetted by the Queen out of milkweed flax. He wished to appear at his ease before the great Rapp, yet he was terribly flustered for fear of a blunder being made in the entertainment. The Queen was pretty and delicate ; her apron had for pockets two wings of the lady-bug.

" ' Let us dance,' cried the young elves.

" ' Not yet,' piped the King. ' Rapp will be here very soon, and you must be ready to make your best bow or courtesy.'

" The little Elf ladies spread their gauzy skirts, and bowed low as Rapp and his Gnomes appeared. Rapp, being in a very good-humor, winked at them, and one cannot expect more notice than that from a prince.

" It was droll to see the Elf King and Queen seated opposite to him at table, he was so much larger than they were. The Elf waiters were obliged to climb silk ladders, which they did as nimbly as spiders.

Rapp was full of his jokes ; he told stories at which the merry elves laughed, like the tinkle of bells, and then he rolled a peach across the board, which knocked the Elf King off his seat.

"A child's voice was heard to join in the mirth this occasioned. Yes, it was a human voice, just beyond the bushes. The elves looked at each other in dismay; Rapp became terribly enraged: his copper face glowed with wrath, his gold hair bristled on end like gilded spikes, and his green eyes flashed fire.

"'What mortal is here?' he cried.

"Then a little girl crept out of the ferns, and stood trembling before him. She had entered a charmed circle without knowing it, and had since watched the elves. She was not like the little girls one sees here now. Her skin was bronze in color, her hair hung down her back straight and black, her feet were shod in moccasins. You only find children like her in the far West—she was an Indian.

"'Why do you disturb our feast, child of man?' asked Rapp, very fiercely. 'I have only to strike the earth, and my servants will carry you away to my palace underground for a hundred years.'

"The child began to cry at this threat, and the elves caught her tears to sprinkle them over the Gnome King's hands, and thus try to soften his heart, which was in reality made of iron.

"'This is my kingdom,' said the Elf King, with dignity. 'You are my guest, King Rapp. The little girl shall not be hurt.'

"'Tell us your story,' said the Queen, kindly.

"'A story! a story!' cried the elves, clustering about the stranger, while Rapp leaned back in his seat, and shut one eye.

" Then the Indian girl told them all about her life. She lived with her tribe down in the valley. Her father had been killed in the chase, and her mother also was dead, so she stayed in the wigwam with her grandmother on the edge of the wood. The chief did not like the hunter's children; he took away the boys to train them for warriors, and he frowned at the girl, so that the old grandmother hid her when the chief stalked past, his feathers and war-paint giving him a savage appearance. Perhaps he did not like the children because their father had been called Big Chief. The old grandmother gathered herbs and simples; she was called to the sick as often as the medicine-men.

" The brothers rode off to earn their first scalp, as they could not be considered heroes until they had killed an enemy; and one day the girl sat weaving her mat in the door of the wigwam, for the Indian women are very industrious. The old grandmother came quickly.

" ' Run to the forest,' she whispered. ' The chief is in a bad humor, and, now your brothers are gone, he sends for you.'

" The girl was in a great fright, the chief was so cruel, and she ran to the forest without once glancing back. Soon she was lost in the cool, green twilight made by the lofty trees; here and there the sunshine shot golden arrows down on her path, revealing mossy nooks where she discovered berries, ripe and dewy, among tangled vines. The flutter of a bird rising from its nest or the crackling of a branch made her heart jump, so much did she dread seeing one of her own people. If one had met her he must carry her back to the chief, or

perhaps suffer death himself. She climbed the mountain to get farther away, her only thought being flight. At last she reached a pool of clear water, high on the mountain-side, where his highness Rapp was taking tea, and she stooped to bathe her face. No sooner had the crystal drops sprinkled her forehead than she sank down on a bed of grass fast asleep. Then the ferns spread their delicate sprays over her, and screened her from sight. She never knew how long her nap might have been had not Rapp's gruff voice aroused her to peep through the foliage at the tea-party in the grotto.

"The little people were interested in the girl's misfortunes. Rapp pretended not to notice, and caught flies, but he really meant to assist her.

"'Go down to my winter palace,' he said to a favorite

Gnome servant, 'and in my dressing-room you will find a winged jacket. Bring it to me.'

" The Gnome servant bowed low, and dived into the earth as a bather dips in the ocean wave. Presently he returned with the winged jacket, which the girl put on.

" ' Now listen to me,' said King Rapp. ' You can fly like a bird in that jacket. If you wish to come into my presence at any time, you have only to clap the wings thrice, like Chanticleer before crowing, and you will be met by a Gnome, who will conduct you to my kingdom. You must go to my chamber, and knock on the steel shield at the head of my bed. Wherever I may be I will answer the summons.'

" The Indian girl thanked the terrible Rapp, and dried her tears. Then the tiny Elf Queen gave her her apron, which grew larger and seemed made of the finest silk.

" ' Whatever article you desire can be had, if you wish with your hand in your pocket,' she said.

" Now the Elf King did not choose to be considered behind the others in kindness, so he took off his slippers, and placed them on the child's feet, which they fitted perfectly.

" ' The Queen can make me another pair,' he said, capering about barefooted. ' You can run miles in those shoes without feeling weary, and the best of it is that they will carry you over the water dryshod.'

" The Indian bid them all farewell, and stepped outside the enchanted circle. Instantly the grotto, the murmuring fountain, the flower-carpet vanished.

" The sun had set, and dark shadows spread along the forest paths as the girl hastened home. She would creep into the grandmother's wigwam in the darkness, and tell her of the fairy gifts she had received. The cruel chief need not be feared when she was the owner of a winged jacket and the elf slippers. If the grandmother thought best, she would go away in the morning, and find another tribe that would treat her kindly.

" When she reached the valley where the Indian settlement was situated it was already night, and so dark that she could not find her wigwam, while she feared to arouse the sleeping natives. Down on the river-bank she saw little lights, bright stars that twinkled, some moving on the water, and others remaining still on the land. This sight puzzled her, and she dreaded to approach near enough to learn what they actually were. While she was wondering, a great boat passed down the river, sparkling all over with colored flame which did not burn, and it panted as it moved like some monster breathing

heavily. It was as large as one hundred canoes put together. The girl held her head in both hands, and crouched down on the ground.

" More wonderful still! On the other side of the river another terrible creature moved quickly along, with a grinding, jarring sound. This one was like a serpent, with links to its body, and it glided over a shining track. The water-demon only puffed as it moved, this other one uttered a shriek that startled all the echoes. The Indian girl hid her face on the bank. She had seen a steamboat and a train of cars.

" These strange sights decided her not to go beyond the edge of the woods until daylight. So she wished for a tent in which to pass the night by putting her hand into the apron pocket. A tent immediately sprang up in the ravine, and when she had entered it she began to feel hungry.

" ' I should like a pot of hominy.'

" Lo! a caldron stood before her smoking with the most delicious hominy, and tasting as if the grandmother had just taken it from the camp-fire. Then she lay down on the ground and slept soundly, until the first beams of the rising sun awakened her.

" The village people were much surprised to see an Indian girl approach, wearing a curious jacket with little wings on the shoulders, and glittering slippers on her feet. She was equally astonished by their white faces and houses. Where was the lodge of the cruel chief? Where were the patches of maize tended by the women? Where was the grandmother?

" ' Have my people gone away? Who has conquered them?'

" But the villagers did not know what she said, and the rude boys formed a ring around her, shouting, 'You are a witch-child! Let's catch her.'

" She sprang high in the air with one bound, spread her wings, and flew away before their eyes.

" The people were greatly excited; they ran about gazing up at the little bird-like form in the sky much as we now look at a balloon; then they ran to the ravine where the beautiful white tent still stood. While they observed it the tent vanished.

" ' She is an Indian witch,' cried the boys.

" ' It is all Rapp and his Gnomes," said an old woman.

" The boys flung burning brands on the spot where the tent had stood, and the witch-child watched the flames kindle as she hovered far above. There was nothing to be done further with the old home; she must search for her own people, and follow them wherever they had gone. She swept along through the air with a delightfully easy motion, and did not mind traversing miles any more than steps on the ground.

" At a great distance from these mountains a toad family lived at the root of an elm-tree. They were yellow and brown and ugly, but according to their own ideas the young lady-toads were quite beautiful. They came forth in the evening to take the air.

" ' Bless my spectacles!' cried the toad mother. ' Here is a witch-child in a winged jacket. Be very pleasant in your manners, children. We shall see if my Lord Rapp is always to have his own way!'

" Then she hopped to the stranger's feet, she having alighted for the night, and said blandly:

E

" ' You must be very tired, my dear.   Have you come far ?'

" ' Yes.   Can you tell me where to find my people ?'

" ' The snail may know.   Stay with us to-night and rest. We are only toads, but we have a guest-chamber.'

" The toad family were so kind that the Indian told them her story ; she so much desired to find her own tribe again.

" The toads blinked and nodded their heads.   The toad mother, after going to the snail which lay in the path, and tapping on its closed door, presently returned.

" ' The snail is a hermit ; it does not go out into society, but likes to stay shut up in its own house.   However, it will ask the night moths, and tell you in the morning.   Now go to bed, darling,' she said.

" The toad guest-chamber was cool and pleasant, for it was the grass around the tree.   They took off the visitor's slippers and apron for her, and tried to coax her out of her jacket as well, but this the witch-child kept on her back.   She was no sooner asleep than the toad mother waddled out to whisper to the little garden-snake :

" ' Run to Mulkgraub as fast as you can, and tell him to meet me at the toadstool turnpike to-morrow.'

" ' I never run—I glide,' said the snake.

" ' Fiddle-de-dee, and don't be silly.   Hurry !' said the toad.

" When the witch-child awoke her lovely slippers and apron were gone, and the toads had also vanished.

" Searching everywhere she came to the marsh.

" ' What is the matter ?' croaked a frog, dressed in green.

" ' The toads have stolen my magic shoes,' she replied.

" ' That is like a toad. You would not catch a frog at such mean tricks. Besides, Mulkgraub pays them.'

" ' Who is Mulkgraub ?' inquired the Indian.

" ' An enemy of King Rapp,' said the frog.

" ' Where can I find my people ?' said the child.

" ' Ask the eagle, if you are not afraid,' returned the frog.

" ' An Indian is never afraid of bird or beast ; it's only those pale faces that change everything,' she said, proudly.

" Then she sought the eagle.

" ' Go toward the setting sun—always westward,' said the eagle. ' Mind that Mulkgraub does not catch you.'

" ' Where does he live ?' inquired our witch-child.

" ' He lives in the water, and he cannot go very far on land. He loves to pour floods over the earth and into Rapp's mines. They are enemies, because Rapp can quench Mulkgraub with fire, so that he becomes a vapor-steam.'

" The witch-child thanked the great eagle and flew on.

" In the meanwhile the ugly old toad mother met Mulkgraub at the toadstool turnpike, and gave him the slippers and apron.

" One would not have believed him so wicked, for he was fair and handsome, with a crown of rushes on his head, and drops of water flowed from his mantle.

" ' Perhaps I may drown out Rapp yet, if the rain only helps me,' he said, and swallowed the slippers and apron as if they had been pills.

" He promised to give a wedding outfit to the toad daughter that married first, and the mother hopped home well satisfied, like the mean old toad she was.

" The second evening the witch-child found a beautiful lady sitting on the border of a lake. She was robed in leaves, and her long hair was also green; but she was altogether lovely, even if her look was sad. She seemed very glad to see the witch-child, and made her sit down beside her, while she held her hand.

" ' I am chained beneath the waters, and can only rise to the surface of the lake,' she said. ' I lived on the mainland very happily until Mulkgraub carried me off in a great storm.'

" ' Let me see your home,' urged the witch-child, curiously.

" ' Mulkgraub might come and find you,' hesitated the lady.

" ' I am not afraid while I wear my jacket.'

" ' Then you must be prepared to live in the water, or the first breath you draw will strangle you.' So saying the lady drew from her girdle a golden clam-shell closed in the form of a bottle, which contained a perfumed liquid. With this she bathed her companion's face, and they dived together into the lake, where the Indian found that she could breathe as easily as in upper air.

"Nothing could exceed the beauty of the prison where the lady lived; certainly Mulkgraub had given her a handsome residence, if he was harsh in other respects. It was a large glass box, with a bell-shaped roof; a broad hall extended from one entrance to the other, but there was not a dark corner in the place where one could hide from the King's searching eye.

"'He is coming,' cried the lady, hiding the witch-child in the folds of her robe. Then, as Mulkgraub entered one door, she darted out of the other, and rising to the lake surface as far as her chain would allow, placed the Indian on shore safely. Once out of harm's way the witch-child began to think of releasing the lady from prison. She must ask King Rapp about the matter. Accordingly she clapped her wings thrice, and a Gnome stood at her elbow.

"'Is King Rapp well?' she asked, politely.

"'Of course,' said the Gnome, gruffly. 'He is made of metal.'

"Then he stamped on the ground, and away they went down dark passages, through caves, past silent pools where the sun never shone—down, down, until it seemed as if they must come out the other side of the world. Here she peeped into vast treasure-houses of rich ore; there she paused before walls of mineral salt; and finally they reached the Gnome palace, where the atmosphere was hot enough to bake one.

" A spacious garden surrounded the palace, with winding paths, arbors, and fountains, and gorgeous birds flitted from tree to tree. All was fresh and sparkling, but even the trees and the fruit on the branches were carved from metals or jewels. The walls of the palace were jasper and malachite, while the floors were solid gold, polished like glass.

" On they went, through the gates and into the palace, coming to the Gnome King's chamber, which had a ceiling of diamond stars, and a bed of silver, fringed and embroidered with pearls. At the head of the bed hung the large shield, and the witch-child tapped on it. Rapp appeared immediately, his eyes greener, his carbuncle nose redder, and his face more like a burnished copper kettle than ever.

" ' I want to help the lady chained in the lake.'

" ' She is an island,' said Rapp. ' When the lake overflowed it made her an island by separation from the mainland.'

" ' Mulkgraub is very wicked to keep her a prisoner against her will,' said the witch-child. ' Please assist me to set her free from his bondage.'

" ' As to that, we are sworn enemies ; my weapon is volcanic fire, and his floods of water. Mulkgraub would make you a slave, if he could, because I helped you ; still, you must remember that he does a great deal of good in the world, as well as some harm.'

" ' What good can he do ?' inquired the witch-child.

" ' He works hard for man, carrying vessels, pushing rafts, and turning mill-wheels. If it were not for my precious metals, he would be of more service than I am. As for this lady island, we must see.'

" Rapp stroked his beard in profound reflection a moment, then struck the steel shield seven times. A peal of thunder seemed to roll over the palace, and a Giant appeared, whose armor resembled dragon scales, with a helmet of brass on his head.

" ' I obey your call, King Rapp,' he said, in a deep voice.

" ' What can restore the island lady to her home ?' asked Rapp.

" ' If she can pour some magic drops into his evening cup of coffee that will make Mulkgraub sleep, I will bring my brother, Fire, to dry the water between her and the mainland, her former home,' said the Giant.

" ' How can the drink be obtained ?' demanded Rapp.

" ' Send a Gnome to the meadow beyond the brook for the herb which has a scarlet flower and blue leaves. Put this into a bottle, which the witch-child will give the prisoner. When Mulkgraub sleeps, the Indian must spring twice over the top of the pine-tree, calling Fire, softly. I will answer.' With this advice the Giant thundered away again.

" Rapp sent for the herb with a scarlet flower and blue leaves, the liquid was distilled into a bottle, and the witch-child once more stood on the ground in the daylight. There was the sad island lady dragging her chain, and wishing herself home on the mainland. She was given the bottle, and quickly told what to do when Mulkgraub came to her glass box for his evening coffee.

" The witch-child hid on the shore, and watched for the signal which was to assure her that Mulkgraub slept. At last the lady rose to the surface and waved her hand. Up sprang the witch-child over the top of the pine-tree, touching the ground on the other side, and rebounding again like an India-rubber ball. ' Fire! fire!' she called very softly, under her breath. Lo! the earth opened and two giant heads emerged; but if Wind, already seen by the girl, was terrible, Fire was more so, for a ruddy glow came from his body, and the grass withered before him. The Giant stood on the bank, and hurled a burning torch into the lake, between the shore and the place where the island was chained, and the torch devoured the water, which rose in a cloud of steam, so that the lady stepped dry-shod back to the mainland.

" Then there was great rejoicing over her return among the rocks and trees, and the witch-child received much praise for her conduct.

" ' There is a storm coming,' shouted Wind. ' I go to share the sport—uprooting trees and whisking off steeples and chimneys.'

" ' As for me, work is never done in the earth,' said Fire.

" Mulkgraub awoke after the mischief was accomplished; the glass box exploded like a soap bubble.

" This is your turn, Rapp,' he said. ' Wait until the spring freshets help me to repay you!'

" Always seeking her tribe and never finding them, the witch-child flew on toward the West. Far below she saw lakes, rivers, and cities; then the wide expanse of prairie became visible, like a sea of waving grain.

" ' This must be the end of the earth,' she thought, and paused.

" It was evening, and the little prairie dogs were sitting on top of their mounds to see what was going on, for they were very curious. When the Indian girl paused to observe them, they gave a shrill bark, and dived out of sight in their burrows.

" ' Can you tell me where to find my people ?'

" At that all the prairie dogs put out their little noses, and one answered—

" ' The red man has gone beyond ; you will find him farther on.'

" ' Always farther on,' sighed the Indian, wearily.

" ' Perhaps you will tell me something I should very much like to know,' said the prairie dog, again perching on his mound. ' If you made a burrow for yourself and family, would you enjoy having a white owl and a rattlesnake come to live with you whether invited or not ?'

" ' I should not,' replied the witch-child.

" ' Look here, then,' and the prairie dog showed her the hole in the ground where it dwelt, and where the owl and the snake would lodge too.

" ' There is room for us all,' said the owl, in a comfortable way, as if the prairie dog's words did not hurt much.

" The witch-child walked forward. The sky seemed to meet the horizon in a flat line before her ; shadows rippled over the ripening acres of corn. She very well knew that her race never planted these fields ; a patch to last one summer satisfied them, and the next year they might select another spot to till. Not a human being was visible ; all the scene was very calm and still.

" At length she reached a stream bordered with cottonwood-trees, and paused to drink. Hither filed a herd of buffalo to slake their thirst.

" ' We know your people well,' they said. ' They hunt and slay us in great numbers. We may be quietly browsing without thought of danger, when the Indians rush down on us like the wind, and hurl arrows at us before we know well what we are about.'

" ' Where shall I find them ?' the girl asked, eagerly.

" ' Farther to the west.'

" The buffaloes thrust their muzzles in the cooling waters, and the witch-child also held her brown hands in the stream.

" ' Mulkgraub, I begin to love you,' she whispered. ' Here you are no longer terrible and mischievous, but give life and refreshment to all creatures.' Then she saw Mulkgraub's fair face laughing up at her from the clear depths, and the next moment her Elf slippers were tossed on the bank. These she put on and ran so swiftly that she seemed a sunbeam chased along the grass by the god of day.

" An emigrant train passed, the white wagons loaded with household furniture ; the mothers and infants riding while the fathers and sons walked before, on the watch for enemies. The route was long and full of danger.

" The witch - child presently heard cries of distress, and mounted on her wings to see what had happened. The emigrants had paused to search for one of their number, a boy who had strayed away. Nothing can be more terrible than to be lost in such a place. If savages find the wanderer, it may be to scalp him or make him a prisoner ; hunger and death come sooner than the savages.

" As soon as she discovered what was the matter, the witch-child flew back, and saw the boy trying to find the path. He felt a hand placed on his shoulder which guided him in the right direction, until he could again behold the white wagons of the emigrants.

" Once more mounting into the sky, the witch-child came to a region of furze, sage, and wormwood, with lofty peaks beyond. She noticed a smoke as of many fires, and her heart bounded with the hope that she had found her tribe at last. Here were lodges and tents, dried venison, and a few horses near ; but the fires came from smouldering ruins of an encampment. There had been a battle between warring tribes, and the place surprised. The witch-child approached sadly, and what do you suppose she found ? A little papoose lying in a folded blanket unharmed. She took it up to kiss, and the baby crowed and smiled. What was she to do with it ? Carrying it on her back, Indian fashion, she climbed the first slopes of the Rocky Mountains, one of King Rapp's homes.

" It was well that she had recovered her Elf slippers, the baby was so heavy she could not fly. Those were happy days ! She fed the little thing with berries, and sang it to sleep, delighted with the pretty brown face and bright eyes.

" One night she reached a house, a lonely ranch of the border settler. You would have mistaken her for a thief to see her steal past the watch-dog into the chamber where the children slept. Beside these white children she laid the Indian baby, the last of its tribe, and went away as noiselessly as she came.

" Fortunately this was a good home for her charge. Next day as she rested at noon, the loud report of a rifle startled her, and a wounded mountain-goat came tumbling down into the valley. She took to her wings in fright; but as she darted up into the air, the sportsman aimed at her, supposing she was some strange specimen of bird. Bang! went the weapon, and she fell. The sportsman hastened to the spot, but found nothing.

" What do you think became of the witch-child ? I believe that King Rapp opened the earth as she sank down, and that she lives with him in the Rocky Mountains to this day."

The Summer Fairy glowed and faded in the radiance of the hearth.

" The witch-child was the last Indian seen in these hills," rustled the other Summer Fairies. " We must always remain as the summer of the year, ranking first in the season, even as the red man came first among human beings here."

" Mousey, I think it is your turn to speak," said the Angora cat, wickedly, and stretched out a paw to the captive.

The little mouse hopped in fear as it answered :

" It is such a strain on my mind to try to think of a story that I shall have a nervous headache for the rest of my life."

" Tut! tut! Remember how sharp my teeth are, and how very unpleasant it is to have one's head nipped off," said the cat.

This made the mouse desperate ; never before had it been

required to do anything but nibble cheese and bacon rind, and now the cruel cat would force it to tell a tale, or be eaten alive.

Nip had sat quietly in Job's hand while the Summer Fairy was talking, and pretended to doze, with his little head sway-ing on one side, like a flower-bell. Now he skipped down, and clasped his arms around the mouse's neck, whispering in its ear.

" Give the mouse time to think," said Nip.

" I give time," interposed the clock, striking violently.

The clock liked none of the company to use the word time besides itself, as it was old and cranky in its ways.

" What change will half an hour make in the mouse's wits ?" growled the cat, and she must have been feeling hungry.

As for Job, he was so much amused by his companions that he could do nothing but look and listen.

" I will tell a story myself, if Queen Puff will stop spinning, so that I may hear myself speak," said Nip.

NIP'S STORY.

"ABOUT the good year 1620 the West Wind stood on her cloud throne, her fair brow wreathed with ivy tendrils, her clear gaze brilliant with untold promises, her stately form erect and instinct with a splendid vitality. She was gazing out over the sea.

"The waves dashed in clouds of spray against granite head-lands, and a dark line of forest extended inland as far as eye could see, unbroken by town or any trace of human life. What was the West Wind looking at? A tiny vessel tossed like a cockle-shell on the billows, and steering timidly across the wide waste of waters. This was the cradle of the queerest baby ever seen.

"Of course, the West Wind knew all about it—this foundling was to be cast on her care and protection. He had no space to grow in the crowded nursery where he was born on the opposite shore of the ocean. The baby's godfather was a great king, but he said, 'Let him go, for he is not like the other children, and will make trouble when he is a big boy.'

"Do you remember the story about the large, ugly duckling among the little ducks and geese of the barnyard that would one day become the beautiful swan? Have you ever heard, Job, that the cuckoo's egg, if allowed to remain in the nest of the hedge-sparrow, crowds out the other nestlings?"

" Yes, I know that," said Job. " Grandfather says"—

" Never mind what Grandfather says," interrupted saucy Nip, reclining on his velvet couch—the mouse's back. " I only intended to make a comparison between the large duckling and the cuckoo and my hero. Well, the king godfather was quite right, for this baby was destined to become a giant, and would have pushed the other children about had it remained at home in the nursery.

" Nearer and nearer came the cradle-vessel while the beautiful West Wind watched. Now there was peril of wreck on the sharp rocks of that stern coast, but the West Wind cast a silk cable and drew it safely to shore. The landing was not too gentle : the infant was drenched in spray, and, emerging gasping from the cold bath, felt a new life tingle in every vein. That was the West Wind's baptism of her charge. Next she smiled and showed him the gifts stored in her mantle, which were to be earned, not given away. A shower of spring blossoms fell softly on the scented air, like a mist of pink snow ; then he saw sheaves of golden grain, then a cluster of purple grapes, with crimson autumn leaves. The infant wanderer, treading for the first time with tender baby feet the soil of a rugged coast, and extending feeble little hands towards these treasures, realized vaguely the greatness of his own destiny.

" How the baby throve, to be sure ! The cold winds swept in from the Atlantic, freezing the spray into icicles to festoon the granite cliffs ; Winter seemed to frown on the stranger, yet he grew.

" Greatest danger of all ! Stealthy forms hovered in the dim,

F

shadowy forest, and glared with looks of hatred at him. Their
faces were dusky in hue—not at all like the baby's fair race—
and they wore gay feathers nodding above their long, black
hair, while their step was as light and swift as that of the shy
wild animals they pursued in the chase. Yes, and these dark
people were not content with frightening the baby by scowling
at him; they gave shrill whoops and cries, and, twanging their
bows, shot arrows at him which pricked smartly. The West
Wind had a cure for these wounds, the balm of courage and
hope.

"I am speaking about the Indians. Perhaps the Summer

Fairies may not like it, but I must tell my story, and they certainly received the baby very rudely."

" How did the baby treat them ?" cried the Summer Fairies.

" We will ask Job's opinion. What if some men came up the mountain and took your house, saying, ' We want to live here ; you can go away.' What would you do ?"

" I would fight 'em," said Job, promptly.

" That is just what the Indians did," said the Fairies.

" But who was this baby ?" asked Job.

" Don't be in such a hurry. The world was not made in a minute," rejoined Nip. " In spite of the Indian enemies, the cold and storms, this sturdy chap flourished, for he was made of the best flesh and blood. The forest cleared a spot here and there, yielding to the strokes of his axe, where the spring blossoms began to bloom on the fruit-trees and shower the grass below instead of remaining hidden in the folds of the West Wind's mantle, and planted grain to ripen under the summer sun for the harvest. The strangest part of it was that the baby was never idle, and his play was always work, building houses out of bits of wood, and making bridges and roads.

" ' Let those play who come after me,' he said, cheerfully.

" So the forests thinned, the dark enemies retreated as the bright daylight followed the path he made, chasing away the gloom of solitude.

" Forward he marched, always following the West Wind, who beckoned him on to fresh exertions, and growing from infancy to childhood as he went on.

" ' Now we will have a city, I guess,' planned the baby. He

began to guess in his very babyhood, and well he might, with a whole new continent before him—all guess-work.

" The West Wind nodded approval, and he built a crooked little town, with narrow, winding streets. How the baby architect enjoyed making the buildings climb steep hills, and then spared fine trees to shade wide avenues, bordered with green turf in the heart of all the crowded town. ' We must have a bit of country here.' So the city was laid out, and the West Wind beckoned him on to build towns and villages, but he cherished his first city with a pride that he never felt in any other, and trotted back, every now and then, to beautify and improve it, which he has continued to do until the present day. The baby grew strong and large—one could see that he would be a towering giant by and by—and his work only grew with him. As he strode on he left Industry spinning many-colored threads in his wake, hammering at forge and anvil, turning great wheels to stir the tranquil rivers, and before him the forests thinned, admitting the sunshine, and the dark enemies melted away, like night shadows, at his approach.

" No obstacle could daunt or discourage him ; the rough path often wounded his feet, his limbs grew very weary, yet where the West Wind led he followed. When he came to broad streams he spanned them with bridges ; he linked miles of space together with an iron band of railway, and then he looped magnetic wires over hill and valley along which thrilled messages as rapidly as the lightning flashes.

" ' Progress !' whistled the locomotive to the earth, and all Industry's wheels turned quicker at the sound ; but the locomotive could not overtake the West Wind or her charge.

" Forward ! ever forward ! The giant youth saw lakes, and launched boats on the clear waters, and then he came to the plains.

" Forward ! ever forward ! The Wind daughter led the way in her chariot of sunset clouds, so that he might hew a path through the wilderness, and earn the treasures she would scatter broadcast. Through deserts of wormwood, beyond crags and cliffs mantled in snow, the giant fought his resolute way, sowing seeds of future growth, finding precious metals, until he reached the shores of another ocean and the Golden Gate.

" In the full radiance of the present, behold him ! He is a giant, but he is not at all handsome ; his features are sharp ; he cares nothing about his dress, or the color of his necktie. He talks through his nose, besides. What name did the West Wind give him ? Not a pretty one, but suited to him — Yankee."

" You are a Yankee, yourself," said Queen Puff, starting her wheel again.

" I am proud of being one. You are a Dutchman," said Nip.

Queen Puff laughed at being called a Dutchman.

" It is true, and I came from Holland in a tile," she confessed.

" I am tired. Take me to ride around the room, Mousey," said Nip.

" I don't know about that," said the cat, suspiciously.

" Only a little ride," urged Nip, looking very roguish all the while. " If you Fairies will make a ring, we can perform circus tricks, mouse and I, equal to those of the Hippodrome."

The others were quite ready for the sport, and soon there was a fairy ring formed on the floor, with Job and the old clock to look down on it. Nip was to have his own way in everything ; they must leave an avenue for the mouse to gallop into the circle in style. " I am clown, ring-master, and rider, all in one. I should like somebody to hold bits of newspaper for hoops for me to jump through, and I will borrow a poppy cloak to leap over. Do I need spurs to make you go ?"

" No, no," hastily squeaked the mouse.

It did Job good to see Nip perform. The mouse went around the circle, with the Fairy dancing on his back, now popping through the paper hoops, now springing over the cloak. At last they paused to rest.

" Let us breathe awhile, and I will show you a trick worth seeing," said Nip.

" Oh, what is it, Nip ? Tell us—do," cried the Fairies.

Nip stood up on the mouse's back once more, and started around the circle, faster and faster, until with one bound they darted out of the ring, and the mouse was safe in its hole before the Angora cat could wink.

" What do you think of that ? I told you it was the best trick of all. Oh, you needn't make big eyes at me, Madam Cat, and curl your whiskers, I am not afraid of you, and the dear little mouse is safe," said Nip.

" If the mouse will join us again, I will promise not to eat it," purred the cat, mildly.

A. Bollett Sc

" Thank you, I will just watch what happens from my hole," replied the mouse, gayly, poking out its head.

" If it is our turn to speak, we will begin," said the Winter Fairies from their perch on the window-sill.

" Yes, do tell me something," said Job, who wished to learn all that the Fairies could impart. " Only I should like to know when my present is to be given."

" Patience," advised the Angora cat.

Then the first Winter Fairy, leaning against the frosted pane, began—

THE GREEN BELT.

" FAR away in the backwoods, where the lumber comes from, a poor widow once lived, with her seven sons, the eldest being eighteen, and the youngest, Peter, a lad of ten years. Peter was born with a caul drawn over his head, like a funny little cap, and the old women said he must meet with great good-fortune in life on this account.

" The father was a hunter, who trapped the beavers and otters, but he had been killed by a fall down a precipice. The winter was very severe, and daily the snow-drifts were piled higher and higher, hedging in the poor cottage from the nearest neighbor, who lived two miles distant.

" One night when a violent hailstorm was dashing torrents of icy musketry upon the roof and against the windows, the family gathered around the fire—there would always be fuel with the forest so near at hand.

" ' It is a great deal to be warm, children,' said the mother, spreading her fingers to enjoy the blaze. ' I must tell you plainly that the meal-chest is nearly empty, and there is but one sack of potatoes left.'

" The children pulled on very long faces ; they began to feel pinched under their jackets with hunger. Just then a distinct tap, tap, was heard on the door.

" ' Can any poor soul be out such a night ?' exclaimed the mother.

" She unbarred the door, and a gust of hail rushed into the room, but on the threshold stood a little old woman shivering with cold. The widow led her to the fire, and at once began to prepare some hot porridge.

" In the meanwhile the children stared at the stranger with eager curiosity. She wore a cloak made of squirrel fur, tied about her throat by the fore-paws ; her face was like a puckered lemon, and her eyes two diamonds, so rapidly did they flash and glitter about the place.

" Peter advanced to her side fearlessly.

" ' Your slippers are dry,' he said.

" ' That is because my shoemaker fits me with pure ice, my dear,' replied the old lady ; then she patted him on the head. ' You are clever because you are a seventh child,' she added ; but Peter did not understand one word of such talk.

" The good mother offered the stranger her own bed, the best she had, and the old woman declared that her fur cloak was a famous couch as she spread it down in one corner, and soon the whole family were asleep. In the morning the old lady had vanished away, and little Peter lay snugly wrapped in the soft fur, with a green belt beside him. Of course, this green belt must be a wonderful gift, and the old lady a fairy ; the family at once decided that to be a fact, yet the belt was so dingy and faded as to seem useless and only fit to hang on a peg behind the door, where it was speedily forgotten. The fur cloak did not vanish away, as they feared it would, and it was afterwards used by Peter for a bed.

" The snow rose higher and higher, and the sun could not warm the keen air. At last there were no more potatoes left in the cottage, and the poor widow was forced to seek some help from her neighbors, even if the way was blocked with deep drifts.

" Night came on, and the mother did not return. She had lost her way, and frozen to death in the bitter cold before she reached the first house. The children watched and waited, then went to bed supperless. It was very sad that the mother must perish thus; but such things happen in the winter every year, especially in the backwoods of which we write.

" Next morning a pretty squirrel rapped on the window-pane with one paw, and when the casement was open hopped into the room quite tamely.

" ' I believe that I will skin and eat you,' said the eldest son, trying to catch the animal.

" ' Not so fast,' chattered the squirrel, leaping nimbly up to a high beam. ' I can do you more good alive I am thinking. Why don't you go out into the world for yourselves?'

" ' I will!' cried the eldest brother, and sprang through the door.

" A bridge of ice reached from the cottage quite to the heart of the forest, and when he stepped on it he found it firm as marble. He soon returned, carrying a beautiful little bird in his hand, which he had found in the path. The bird had a crest of scarlet feathers on its head, while the wings were velvet black.

" ' If you make a nest for the bird, it will lay a pearl egg every day,' said the squirrel.

" ' Let me see what I can do,' said the second boy, encouraged by his brother's success; so, crossing the ice-bridge, he disappeared.

" When he came back he carried a copper porridge-pot, which was so brightly polished that it resembled gold. The hungry children found a handful of meal, and made porridge in the new vessel. When they poured out the porridge, the pot was again full.

" ' It will always be filled whenever emptied,' said the squirrel, also tasting the dish daintily.

" ' Hurrah! We shall never be hungry after this,' said the second son, hugging the pot in his arms.

" Then the third son crossed the ice-bridge, and in less than five minutes appeared with a silver gridiron.

" ' Who would like a cake baked on my gridiron?' he asked.

" No sooner was one cake taken, crisp and brown, from the fire than another lay in its place, and the gridiron did not cease from cooking until the children were well filled. It must have taken a great many cakes to make a boy say he had eaten enough!

" Then the fourth boy said, ' I will try my luck;' and crossed the bridge as the others had done.

" He found a tiny cask made of rough iron, but it was always filled with rare, sweet wine, and the supply could never fail.

" The fifth son in his turn found nothing but a delicate white cloth hanging upon a tree. He entered the cottage with a doleful face and slow step. His portion was only a cloth, when his brothers had found a bird that would lay pearl eggs, a porridge-pot always full, a silver gridiron, and a cask of wine.

" ' Spread the cloth on the table,' said the squirrel.

" Fancy their astonishment when a grand feast appeared on the magic cloth. Ducks and turkeys dressed with flowers, delicious confectionery in sparkling heaps, and tempting fruits. The fifth boy's gift was not so poor a one after all.

" Then the sixth son walked out, and directly before him lay a beautiful gold trumpet. He blew a loud blast, and immediately all animals responded to the summons—bears, monkeys, jaguars, moose, and deer, even wild cats.

" ' Eat us up, if you like, or do anything with us ; we are your slaves,' growled the animals together.

" Yes, he had control over all beasts for any service he might require.

" ' The little old woman must have been a fairy after all !' shouted the brothers, beside themselves with delight.

" The pretty squirrel sitting up on the beam with its tail curled over its back was the fairy all the while.

" ' What am I to own ?' asked Peter, in dismay.

" The seventh son went out across the ice - bridge and

searched every path, gazing eagerly up into the trees ; but he found just nothing at all. The brothers, in their own joy, scarcely noticed poor Peter's disappointment.

" ' I must seek my fortune out in the wide world,' said the eldest, taking the scarlet bird in his hand ; then with a careless good-bye he was gone.

" The others quickly followed, until Peter was left alone.

" The little squirrel leaped down, and nestled close beside the weeping child.

" ' Dry your tears ; you are the seventh child, and therefore the most fortunate of all. Here is the caul with which you were born, to hang about your neck, and that will bring good luck. The green belt is your gift.'

" The squirrel had the same clear diamond eyes that the old woman possessed who visited their cottage on the stormy evening.

" Peter took the belt from the peg where it had hung, and, behold ! it was bright in color, and bore these lines—

> ' You shall have power to change your shape,
>   To Lion, Tiger, Dog, or Ape ;
>   To help the good, torment the bad,
>   To make some gay, and others sad.'

" Peter danced for joy, and the squirrel skipped also on its hind feet to keep him company.

" ' Put the caul on your head, and you will see just what your brothers are doing, wherever they go,' said the squirrel.

" Peter held the dried skin-cap over his head, and shut his eyes. The first son travelled far, still holding the scarlet bird in his hand. He entered a city in the East, where there were mosques with glittering domes, palaces, and bazaars. In the harbor queerly shaped boats darted about, and the stately ships had the flags of all nations floating from their masts.

" The first son crossed the court of a magnificent building, led by black slaves in gorgeous turbans and robes, and entered a marble-paved hall adorned with pillars and sparkling fountains, where a prince sat on his throne, and he bowed low before him. The prince admired the little scarlet bird, as a prince has a right to admire a new toy, and he gave to the owner ten chests of gold coins, a house to live in, and three trained Arabian horses from the royal stables in exchange for it.

" ' My eldest brother will pass his days in idleness and ease,' said Peter. ' He will doze on velvet cushions, be refreshed with delicate perfumes, and smoke a pipe mounted with gems and amber. His raiment will be the finest linen, the softest satin and damask. He will forget entirely that he was ever a poor boy living in the woods.'

" ' So much for him. Now for the next one.' The squirrel fairy was very polite in listening to the history, although it knew already everything that would happen,. Peter must learn to like his gift the best, and so he was to see his brothers first.

" The second son was walking along the road where the hedges were in bloom and the fields ready for the harvest. He was ruddy and strong-limbed, as well he might be, for the porridge-pot never failed. At the farm-house door stood a pretty maid, as the crimson sunset turned every object to red and gold. She was calling the harvest-laborers to their supper by blowing through the horn; and the second son, coming among the rest, loved her for her sweet smile and light footstep as she waited on the table.

" ' It will be love in a cottage,' said Peter. ' They need never suffer from hunger while they keep the porridge-pot.'

" ' Who comes next ?' inquired the squirrel.

" The third and fourth brothers were together in the city of Paris, one with his silver gridiron and the other with his table-cloth, which was always covered with dainties. That was a famous partnership ! They had a cook-shop, called a *café*, with tables and waiters. Even great noblemen came to taste of the cakes baked on the gridiron ; and where the nobility lead, common people must follow the fashion, like one sheep after another.

" The fifth son, no less fortunate than his brothers, drew sweet wine from the tiny cask, and built a warehouse in which to store his barrels. The fame of his wine went everywhere, the flavor was so delicate, because it was made from fairy grapes, and no one could tell the vintage.

" The sixth son went to the South American pampas, where he gathered immense flocks, for all he had to do was to blow through the trumpet, and cattle followed the sound.

" ' I would not choose the place of any of them,' said Peter, and the squirrel fairy was pleased with this decision. They left the cottage to visit the Fairies, and in the depths of the forest the snow had melted away like magic, as if for the tiny people to hold their sports. The squirrel here became a fairy lady no longer than one of Peter's fingers, and her companions,

dressed in green, so that they resembled moving leaves, welcomed her back cordially.

"'I was the old woman and the squirrel too,' she laughed.
'I take those forms for travelling about.'

"'Your eyes are still diamond clear,' said Peter, and then
he thanked her for all the kindness she had shown to his
family.

"'We trained the bird and made all the other gifts,' cried
the Fairies. 'Then we placed them in the path.'

"Peter seated himself on the grass to watch the Fairies
dance; they spun around in giddy circles without losing their

breath, until it made the boy's eyes ache to look at them. The
fairy music was wonderful, the wee musicians being ranged
around a toadstool upon which stood the leader, and they blew
through dandelion stems for instruments.

" When they ceased dancing they all clustered about Peter, and the squirrel fairy sat on his shoulder. One little sprite had a tiny broom made of thistle, and a dust-brush under one arm, with which she dusted and swept the flowers surrounding the fairy circle, until not a speck of dust remained. This sprite had a sharp nose and a prim little waist. One could plainly see that she was set in her ways.

" ' I am a household spirit, and my name is Pucker. I steal through the keyhole of the silent houses at night, and if I find the rooms untidy, I nip the housemaid in her sleep until she is black and blue. I am very severe on housekeepers. If I discover the dishes improperly washed, or egg-shells and bones lying about in the humblest cottage, I tweak the good wife's nose, and box her ears soundly. Every one can be clean, and they must be happier for neat homes. I stand no nonsense ' —and the brisk little Pucker began to dust the flowers again with renewed energy, until the roses and pinks blushed a deeper red from sheer anger.

" ' Will you let our beautiful faces alone ?' they exclaimed.

" ' My name is Gull,' said a merry, romping fairy, dancing on a spider-web bridge. ' I love to play tricks better than to work. I steal cream and sugar from the closet, and whisk away the glass of water just as a body is about to drink—that is capital fun !'

" ' I am Grim,' said a short, stout elf with a droll face. ' I pull the master's beard, and throw him into ditches by the roadside when he comes home from the public - house at night. He may lie there until morning, yet I give him no rest ; he is pricked with nettles, pounded with sharp stones, and his boots filled with cold water—that is the way to cure drunkards.'

" Peter rose at last.

" ' I could stay with you forever, dear Fairies, but I must start on my travels.'

" Leaving the forest, he saw three graceful horses in a meadow, now prancing forward with manes and tails streaming on the wind, now bounding high in the air to vault over the boundary wall.

" ' I should like to be a horse,' thought Peter.   Immediately he began to prance too—his coat of the softest black color, his limbs delicately rounded, and his hair like spun silk.   A golden bridle hung over his arched neck, and his hoofs were also shod with shining gold.   The young farmer who owned the meadow saw the horse nibbling grass, and apparently as tame as a kitten.   Although so rich and owning already many steeds, he was always envious of other people and their possessions.

" ' Who has a horse so much more beautiful than any of mine ?' he inquired, frowning angrily.

" He advanced towards Peter, and, as no one seemed to claim the animal, he determined to have it at all hazards.   He just touched the golden bridle, when Peter shook his head saucily, and danced away.   The farmer ran faster after the stranger horse, bewitched by its beauty, and Peter played all kinds of pranks.   At last he stood still, and the farmer, overjoyed at such unexpected docility, mounted, when away dashed Peter as swift as an arrow shot from a bow, the rider clinging to his back.   Peter enjoyed the race ; but when he reached the bank of a river he determined to punish the envious farmer still further, so he plunged into the stream, wished himself a fish, and slid away from under the rider, leaving him floundering in deep water.

" ' Perhaps that will teach him a lesson,' said Peter, watching the farmer climb the bank again.

" Then he swam to the opposite shore, and became a boy, with his green belt around his waist.

" Presently he came to a house, where all was silent except the cackling of the fowls in the barn-yard. The door stood wide open, and on the step lay the dog winking lazily in the sun. Peter boldly entered, and in the corner he found a young girl sitting alone, with a pile of flax on the floor and her spinning-wheel before her.

" ' Why do you stay in the dark corner ?' asked Peter.

" ' Because every one has gone to the county fair, and left me alone,' sobbed the girl. ' My mistress said I could not leave until my work was done, and she very well knew that I could not finish it before nightfall. Oh! I want to see the fat cattle and the big vegetables, the bedquilts and prize bread, so much !'

" Peter just stepped forward and kissed her on both eyelids, and she fell asleep.

" ' I want the Fairies,' whispered the boy.

" Through the window they fluttered like a cloud of brilliant butterflies. No need to tell them what to do; for Pucker set to work on the wheel, which whizzed around without making the least noise, and the threads were wound off by no less nimble fingers. Fairy Grim, having no drunken men to trip up, began to sort the flax, and Fairy Gull dressed the sleeping girl by changing her cotton gown to cashmere, and twining bright ribbons in her hair. How surprised she was when she opened her eyes five minutes later to find the work neatly finished, herself gayly dressed, and a donkey standing before the door, with a saddle of red leather trimmed with bells on his back, ready to carry her to the fair!

" This donkey was our friend Peter; and when the poor girl had mounted his back, away he trotted as fast as his four little legs would carry him. He did not allow himself to show any ugly donkey tricks, such as lying down to roll in the dust, or shying at a stream of water. When they reached the borders of the town, he left the girl to go on alone, and became a boy, as he did not like the donkey character much.

"After that Peter became a madcap, if ever there was one. He blew out the farmers' pipes, overturned the hay-mounds, tied the dairymaids to the cows' tails, and set all the dogs crazy. Then he went to a city, where he was one day a chimney-sweep, scrambling through the flues and sprinkling soot down to make people sneeze, and an organ-grinder the next. He pretended to be a beggar with one leg; he pulled door-bells and ran away; he laid traps for thieves, so that the police seized them. All this Peter called seeing life; yet he soon grew weary of it. He went back to the forest to see the squirrel fairy; and when he entered the familiar path she ran to meet him gladly. Although Peter had been gone many years, the squirrel was as young as ever, with the sparkling diamond eyes.

"'It is time you did something better than cut capers. I will tell you what to do — you should win glory as a soldier, and there will soon be a war across the seas.'

" So Peter went across seas; and he had no sooner set foot in

a foreign land than he heard that the Emperor of the country had declared war on a neighboring Prince. Peter bought a field of carrots, and when they were ripe he changed them into an army of splendid soldiers, and placed himself at the head in a gold uniform to match the yellow colors of the regiments.

" ' We serve under the Emperor,' he said, drawing up his men before the Imperial Palace.

" ' Will you charge the enemy now?' asked the Emperor.

" ' The sooner the better,' returned the brave Peter. ' The troops will not wither then; and if they do fall, they are only vegetable men after all,' he added to himself.

" Peter and his carrot soldiers attacked the enemy with tremendous vigor, so that they were driven at the point of the bayonet into the river, their only choice being to jump into the water or become spiked on the weapons like cockchafers.

" After the engagement the carrot troops retired into the forest, where they died, and the Fairies buried them in consideration of their valiant deeds.

" Peter was created commander-in-chief of the Imperial forces, as he was flesh and blood instead of carrot. Of course he could not be made commander-in-chief without stepping into some other man's shoes. General Rub-a-dub did not like the change at all. He declared that if the Emperor would only have given him time he could have dug trenches about the enemy, attacked them by flank movements and other military tactics, until they were safely bagged, every soldier of them, instead of giving Peter all the glory.

" ' Where are your troops?' asked General Rub-a-dub, before the Emperor himself.

" ' They disbanded in the woods,' said Peter.

" ' I saw nothing but a pile of carrots,' retorted General Rub-a-dub. ' I believe your soldiers were nothing but carrot men after all.'

" ' Nonsense !' cried the Emperor, growing purple in the face with wrath at the idea of his empire being defended by an army of carrots. ' If I believed half that you say, Rub-a-dub, I would command that every carrot in my dominions should be pulled up by the roots, and no more be planted for one while.'

" ' I will execute the wise order, if it please your majesty,' General Rub-a-dub hastened to reply. ' Without his carrots, you will find that your new commander-in-chief is not much of an officer.'

" Peter was at his wits' end ; but a wasp flew past, and buzzed in his ear :

" ' We will use beets.'

" The neighboring Prince gathered new forces, and marched into the Emperor's territory, blowing trumpets under his majesty's nose. General Rub-a-dub drilled his men, and watched Peter quite fiercely, twirling his mustache. At the very last moment, when the enemy was preparing to besiege the Imperial city, Peter stole softly out to the Fairies, and they employed countless numbers of owls and bats to pull up all the beets in the kingdom, and bring the vegetables to the edge of the wood.

" When the next morning's sun rose, Peter turned all the beets into soldiers, and marched to join the Emperor's army. The beet soldiers were infinitely more splendid in appearance than the carrots had been ; they were glowing crimson not only in uniform, but their faces were of the same hue, and their caps were green, with nodding plumes. Peter wore a costume of crimson velvet to match his troops, studded with rubies, and his sword-hilt was incrusted with the same jewels.

" Peter told the Emperor that he believed in sudden action and quick movements, like Napoleon. He knew well that the vegetable men could not press the siege, as they would wither by sundown, if exposed to intense heat.

" ' General Rub-a-dub is an old fogy in his ideas,' whispered Peter in the Emperor's ear, and the Emperor nodded his head.

" If the carrot soldiers had fought well, the beet men did ten times better ; and when they were slashed down, they shed real blood-beet juice. The enemy was again driven back with terrible slaughter, and the beet men dragged themselves to the wood, where the Fairies buried them. Rub-a-dub was not satisfied. Peace was, indeed, restored to the country ; still it was all done through the tricks of the new commander-in-chief, he declared.

" ' There is not a ripe beet left in the kingdom,' complained this general. ' Your last army was beet men.'

" ' How !' cried the Emperor. ' Shall I be deprived of my favorite salad because the beets are gone ?'

" Peter was again bewildered. The wasp buzzed in his ear—

" ' We must use radishes next time.'

" So when the warlike Prince, having been twice defeated, induced two other Princes to join him in fighting against the Emperor, Peter brought an overwhelming force of radishes, some in scarlet jackets and others in bright yellow, to the rescue. The radish troops were more spirited than the carrots or beets had been, perhaps because radishes are so peppery. Peter charged at their head, this time using a silver sword, with an edge like a razor, and a shield against which blows fell harmless. The three Princes fled before the valiant radishes; but the latter withered in the hot sun, after the victory, before they could seek the forest shade, and lay in rows along the highway —nothing but wilted radishes.

"'They were radishes,' said General Rub-a-dub, scornfully. The Emperor patted the commander's shoulder graciously.

"'If vegetable soldiers can defend my dominions so bravely without loss of human life, I shall always employ them. I implore you not to use beets in the future, and deprive me of my favorite salad. I make you chief for life.'

"'If it please your majesty, I must now return home,' said Peter, bowing low before the throne. 'Your army can be made of real men by General Rub-a-dub.'

"Then Peter crossed the seas once more, and lived in the very cottage where he was born. He hung the green belt on

the peg behind the door; and if you had happened to pass the place, you would have seen a quiet old man, with a squirrel perched on his shoulder. The squirrel had diamond clear eyes."

The Winter Fairies clustered against the frosted pane like snow-flakes.

"All the same, I should like my present," said Job. "When *will* the Fairy of the Cascade come?"

"You must not be so impatient," rejoined the Angora cat. She had shown her good-breeding by turning her back on the mouse's hole, and behaving as if she had forgotten all about it, although the mouse's nose did look tempting.

"What do you suppose the gift is?" asked Queen Puff.

"I can't guess," said Job, staring at the fire with bright eyes, and nursing his knee. "Is it a top?"

"No."

"A ship?"

"No."

"Oh, oh!—A kite?"

"No."

Something very odd happened. After his circus pranks with the mouse Nip had been flying around the room. At last he came to Job's picture-gallery. Now I suppose you imagine that Job was too poor to have a picture-gallery; but he owned a very good one. The previous summer he had stood by the roadside when a Mountain-House coach came down the hill, crowded with people, and a golden-haired little girl nodded to Job in a friendly way—"Would you like a paper, boy?"

Before he could reply the golden head vanished, the coach lumbered on, and he held a " Harper's Weekly " in his hand. What delight the pages afforded simple Job! He ran home and cut out the pictures with Grandfather's shears, then fastened them on the wall with large crooked pins. There were four big prints, and ever so many little ones, which afforded a good variety for a gallery. Here was a queer old negro mend-ing a shoe at the door of his shop; there a beautiful lady, with a high satin ruff about her neck and pearls in her dark hair. The gems of the collection were the two largest woodcuts, according to Job's ideas, and one of these was a palace, with gables and pointed roof, and the other a beach, where a fisherman's wife waited for the boats to come in.

Nip had bewitched these pictures, and he now sat on the pin that held the palace to the wall.

The old negro cobbler in the shop door began to work—tap, tap sounded his hammer; while the parrot in the cage above scolded a monkey that was slyly stealing its food.

Then the beautiful lady smiled, showing her white teeth, and unfurled her large fan—one could see that she was a Spaniard from the grace with which she used it. As for the fisherman's wife, she took several steps along the beach, shading her eyes with her hand, and the white sails gleamed off the bar. The fishing fleet was coming in safely after the storm.

"Now look at the palace," said Nip, from his seat on the large brass pin.

THE HOUSE THAT JACQUES BUILT.

"I AM very old," said the Palace in the picture. "There are no such strong walls and towers built nowadays, because there are no robber bands to plunder as they did when I was erected; and great armies are not as likely to besiege and destroy cities.

"Yes, I am very old, as I said before, and Jacques Cœur built me after the quaint fancy of his own mind. I suppose there never was a palace with as many odd twists and turns in it as I have.

"Do you know who Jacques Cœur was? He lived in France a great many years ago, and he was called the merchant prince of his country. He was a good and wise man, but his king was weak and cruel, and made him suffer for his prosperity. Those were the days when Joan of Arc saved France, but Jacques Cœur helped with his money.

"He built his home in the old city of Bourges, which had narrow, winding streets, where the tall buildings seemed to touch overhead, and a grand cathedral stands now just as it did in Jacques Cœur's day.

"Here you see the front of the palace, which opens on the street. The wall is richly carved, and the massive gateway has a large knocker on the door, with a hammer that strikes on a heart. To the left is a pointed tower, evidently belonging to the kitchen. Over the kitchen door funny little figures are carved of cooks and scullions busy with brooms and pots, just like cooks at the present time.

" The rear of the building is like a fortress, with a rampart and moat, and no windows. There is a round tower overlooking the moat, where Jacques Cœur had an office; and above the office was a vaulted strong room, secured by an iron door, and a wonderful lock, that still works after centuries of use. There he kept his money-bags. There were no safes or police then, and the burglars were armed bands of rude soldiers.

" More than four hundred years ago Jacques Cœur stood in this little office, looking through the narrow window out on the roofs and chimneys, which were ornamented with gilded cockle-shells and statues of monks. His thoughts must have wandered beyond the moat and the level meadows of the province of Berri to the blue Mediterranean, where every breeze was wafting along his ships freighted with wealth from the rich ports of the East. He would serve his king, Charles VII., faithfully; but the wicked monarch would pay the debt by arresting the merchant and casting him into prison.

" Jacques Cœur belonged to the people. His father was a merchant before him, but the son had greater industry. He sent out travellers in every direction; he regulated the mint of Paris; he went on a mission to the Pope. When he erected this palace, he said to himself:

" ' This house shall be my tomb, and tell the story of my life and age. I have earned my gold by working hard—yet it is not safe for me to be rich; so I must make iron doors and secret passages, as well as drawing-rooms and chapels, decorated by

Italian artists. Every one shall know that here lived a great merchant, with wife, sons, and a daughter. He loved Bourges, and Bourges loved him, for he paid his workmen well. My motto is a good one — " To a brave heart nothing is impossible." '

" Here I stand and still tell the story," said the picture, and became silent.

Queen Puff was working with all her tiny might.

" Dear Job, I must finish the children's dreams for Christmas Eve," said the good little thing. " I have a story to tell when I get through with the thread."

" Take your own time," interposed Nip, swinging his heels on the pin, as if it had been a cross-bar. " I will give you some of my own experience. I went last year to see a fairy regatta, and will tell you all about it."

H

THE FAIRY REGATTA.

" I BELIEVE that you are all aware of my place of residence. I live in the Berkshire Hills, behind a blackberry-bush; and you may always leave word if I am wanted with the grasshoppers near by, for my trade as pedler naturally keeps me absent a good deal.

" Well, I thought I knew the country pretty well, but last summer I made a discovery. To tell the truth, I had been teasing a blackbird, and I told him if I could discover his nest I would frighten his wife into fits. This was only talk, as my heart is in the right place, after all; still I must peer about in search of the nest, to torment the bird.

" Suddenly I found myself at the mouth of a cave—that was my discovery. I never saw the cave before. The entrance was so high and wide that it seemed as if a ship might pass in without touching the lofty arches. I walked in and soon found that the cavern narrowed more and more; at the farther extremity there was a mere crack, through which I slipped, and groped my way onward. It was very dark until a turn in the passage showed a ray of light in the distance, and I also heard the murmur of water trickling along a rocky bed beside me. The light increasing, I soon found myself on the brink of a small lake, and on the margin where the rushes grew was moored a little boat of silver, with two oars just large enough

for my grasp. Could anything have been more delightful!
The boat seemed waiting for me. Whether it was or not, I
lost no time in jumping aboard, and pushing off from the shore.
I have a great deal of curiosity, and I like to see every place
with my own eyes. No guide-books of travel for Nip, if you
please!

"The radiance resting on the lake was like moonlight, and
as my boat floated along I noticed that the water was quick-
silver, and the lilies on the surface large pearls with emerald
leaves. I rowed swiftly in one direction, and then concluded
to change my course; but when I attempted to turn the boat
around, I discovered that it was drawn straight on as a steel
obeys the magnet. This surprised me, but I was not afraid.
' I suppose I must be going to the opposite shore for some

good purpose, whether I wish to or not,' I reflected. The boat was borne along by the current to an island in the middle of the lake, where stood a single tree covered with scarlet blossoms of great beauty. Out I skipped to examine the strange tree, and immediately my boat vanished. A winding staircase of polished brass led around the trunk of the tree, and I climbed it, as there seemed nothing else to do. When I gained the top, one of the scarlet blossoms unfolded into a red-velvet arm-chair; and I had no sooner seated myself in it than the whole island began to sink slowly below the surface of the lake, carrying me down miles into the depths of the earth. When we stopped, the scarlet blossom puffed me away with a breath of wind like a feather, and I landed on my feet. Here was another cave, only one altogether splendid, for the walls were veined with rough gold ore, and a diamond chandelier sparkled in the dome. Purple-velvet curtains, fringed with gold, shaded the entrance, and two curious vases stood on each side. I was greeted by an old magician, with a white beard, who had a skull-cap on his head.

" 'I own all this region,' he said. 'Have you come to join in the Fairy Regatta, little man?'

" 'I suppose so, since I am here,' I replied. 'I can never win, though, I fear.'

" 'We shall see;' and the magician led me away from the cave down to the bank of a stream, where a multitude of little boats were darting about, some fashioned like swans, others like dolphins and crabs, guided by the Nixies' tiny water-spirits.

" 'The Nixies have an annual regatta at this spot,' explained the kind magician. 'Their Queen is seated under a rose-leaf

pavilion over yonder, and she will give as a prize the magic drum.'

"He then took from his snuff-box a boat made in the form of a dragon-fly, with outspread wings, which was cut from a single sapphire. He launched me in this boat, first giving me three grains of snuff to use if I found it necessary. Away I sped in my lovely dragon-fly boat to form in line with five others; and the Nixy boatman could not object to my trying my luck with the rest, as the powerful magician had sent me to join in the race.

" The first boat was a ruby grasshopper, on the wherry model; the second, a pearl snail-shell, of the dory style; the third, a crystal spider; the fourth, a miniature ebony shark; and the fifth, a goldfish.

" The Nixy Queen, seated beneath her rose-leaf pavilion, bowed to the magician on the opposite shore, and gave one tap on the magic drum, as a signal for the race to begin. Away shot the little boats, the oars flashing through the water, and made for the goal, a cork anchored in mid-stream for a buoy.

" The grasshopper boat was named the *Dauntless*, and its colors were green.

" The pearl snail-shell was christened *Vixen*, with a white badge.

" The crystal spider had *Mermaid* written on the stern, and sported pink.

" The ebony shark was *Sea Foam*, with dark blue.

" As for my dragon-fly, I dubbed it *Nip the Second*, with orange colors, as I am so fond of yellow.

" At the tap of the magic drum we got off in good order, the *Dauntless* leading, *Mermaid* second, *Vixen* and *Sea Foam* in line. The Nixies showed good training, and their Queen was delighted with their fine appearance. As for me, it was plainly to be seen that they considered me of no great account, and not likely to prove a rival. I thought, ' It is a good old proverb that says let him laugh who wins.'

" The *Dauntless* had got the lead, which is an advantage, and meant to keep it; but I made a fine spurt, and drew alongside of the Nixy fleet. I could never have kept pace with them had I not scattered the three snuff-grains given me by the magician. This had a very curious effect on my companions—each Nixy rested on his oars, bowed his head, and sneezed.

" I pulled away while this happened, and gained the cork in advance of the *Dauntless* by two boats' length. That was a victory! And the contest was most exciting.

" I received the magic drum, which was no larger than a thimble, and could be slung over the shoulder with a chain. What do you suppose I did with it? Why, I beat one smart tune on it, and sold it to the Nixies, who were anxious to keep it in their possession. Heigh! I almost wish that I had kept it, for I believe I could have got more for it above ground, if only as a curiosity.

" I went back to the magician, who entertained me very handsomely, for he was pleased with my success. He wished me to remain with him down there in the gold cave, and promised to tell me half of his secrets, which were written on parchment in a great book fastened with a steel lock; but I missed my dear home behind the blackberry-bush. I sang 'Home, sweet home,' to the magician; and after that he made no objection to my departure, partly because I sang it out of time, I believe.

" He took his large pipe with the porcelain bowl, and when he had lighted it he told me to step into the pipe, and he would blow me up to the earth's surface.

" ' I am afraid of getting burned,' I objected.

" ' I would not hurt you for the world,' said the magician; and I must say he was as good as his word.

" He rubbed some sweet ointment over me to keep my skin from scorching, and while he was doing it he picked my pocket

of the sum I had received from the Nixies for the magic drum.
I did not discover this until I was home; but I call it mean,
as it was a fair trade. So I was popped into the porcelain bowl
of the pipe, the magician blew a cloud of smoke, and away I
went up to the earth's surface and daylight again."

Job was much amused at the idea of Nip rowing a match.

"Do you believe you would have won without the snuff?"

"I daresay I could with practice," said Nip. "You should
have seen the Fairy Regatta in line, though!"

"I wish you had kept the drum," said Job.

"So do I. Perhaps I will go to the match next year. I
don't mind telling you that I practice every spare moment in
a walnut-shell which I keep in the horse-trough."

Fairies may have plans for the future, just as mortals say
"I will go to a new school in the spring." Queen Puff had
finished her dream-thread by this time, and set aside her wheel.

"The last of it will serve for morning dreams just before the
children awake to look into their stockings," she said, smoothing her apron and folding her hands in her lap.

Then all kept silence while she told the following story.

THE DOVE MAIDEN.

"A LITTLE boy and girl were trudging home from school, swinging their luncheon basket between them. The little girl's face was pretty and good-humored; the boy had an ugly habit of frowning and shutting his mouth firmly when anything did not please him. The sister had only to find the largest slice of buttered bread in the luncheon basket to bring this ugly scowl; and the good schoolmistress said that Otto would make neither a kind nor generous man if he did not mend that troublesome temper of his own.

"The evening was clear and beautiful. You never saw a country like that through which these children walked, Job. The land was very level, and protected by dikes from the overflow of the sea. The meadows were rich with grass and wild flowers, where large herds of sleek cattle fed; and canals wound in and out among these fields, with barges floating along on their clear waters. If you were not an ignorant boy, Job, you would know at a glance that this country was Holland, where the first

Dutch settlers of New York came from, even as Nip's Yankee giant landed on the coast of New England. The boy and girl, Otto and Sophia Snyder by name, had entered the wide meadow which alone separated them from their home.

" ' Let us rest awhile,' said Otto, throwing himself on the ground ; and Sophia followed his example.

" The grass rose like a green sea all about them. Over against the sky was the neat village where they lived, the red-roofed houses shaded by willow-trees. Otto knew Aunt Katrine would expect him to feed the hens and pigs, as well as to drive the cows home ; still he sat in the grass.

" They talked about the beetles toiling at their feet, the bustling, hurrying ants, and Otto tried to catch a pretty field-mouse that darted past him to hide in the ground.

" ' If I could find the nest, what fun it would be to take the baby mice !' exclaimed the boy, crawling along on his hands and knees to the spot where the mouse had disappeared.

" Three storks were roaming by the water-side, among flags and osiers, in search of frogs.

" ' Oh, Otto ! look up there !' cried Sophia, pointing to the sky.

" Otto forgot the hunted mouse in a moment, and sprang to his feet to gaze in the direction indicated by his sister. High up in the air were two doves, with feathers of dazzling whiteness, that soared along unconscious of danger. A large black hawk was winging its swift flight in keen pursuit of the pretty doves. At last the birds seemed to become aware of their peril, for the hawk darted above them, prepared to swoop down on the helpless mates. The children, who had watched their movements with breathless interest, now saw them circle nearer and

nearer to the earth in their terror of the cruel enemy in pursuit.

" 'Dear little birds, I will shelter you,' cried Sophia, holding out her apron in her eagerness to save them.

" The doves sank into the apron, exhausted with fatigue and fear, and the girl clasped them in her arms. The hawk dashed down until his sharp beak and glittering eyes were close to Sophia's face ; and she screamed with terror, but she did not drop the doves.

" Now came the ugly frown on Otto's face ; he seized a stick, and aimed a blow at the bold hawk.

" 'The doves belong to us ! Let me see you touch them !' he shouted, angrily.

" The hawk gave a hoarse shriek of rage and disappointment, then rose slowly in the air, and flew away in search of other game. The children cautiously uncovered the birds to admire them, and Otto held one while Sophia carried the other. Never were such lovely birds seen ! Their plumage was snowy on the wings, and shaded to crimson and emerald green on the breasts. Around each slender neck was fastened a gold chain studded with jewels, which flashed in the sun like a circlet of fire.

" The captives were restless to resume their flight after the danger was over; but the children had no idea of losing such charming pets, so they carried them home in spite of their frantic efforts to escape.

" The village was as clean as constant scrubbing by the tidy housewives could make it. You should have seen Aunt Katrine, rain or shine, polish the door-step, just as they do still in the city of Philadelphia. The village people were already drinking tea, after the day's labors, and the children passed open doors, which afforded glimpses of tables, shelves, and earthenware, all spotlessly pure.

"Aunt Katrine was surprised to see the prizes the children had captured at the expense of being late to supper. She put on her spectacles, and held up her hands. 'I never saw doves with chains around their necks,' she declared.

"'I shall take mine off,' said Otto, resolutely.

"He untwined the chain, and the dove immediately changed to a little girl, with soft brown hair, her dress of some delicate fabric, like a cobweb, embroidered with silver stars, with silver shoes on her feet, and a cap of silver on her head. She was unlike any one that Aunt Katrine had ever seen, and the children thought her an angel.

"The other dove no sooner beheld the transformation of its mate than it gave a loud note of alarm, and, slipping through Sophia's fat fingers, soared high in the air. Sophia was staring so earnestly at the stranger child that she did not recover her wits until her pet was out of reach.

"The dove child, remaining below, gazed about wonderingly for a moment, then sprang up into the air, and tried to snatch the chain from Otto's grasp. She nearly succeeded in doing so, but the boy was larger and stronger, and held it in his grasp.

"'This belongs to me, and you do, too,' he said, frowning. 'When I am a man I shall take the chain to Rotterdam, and sell it for a pot of money.'

"Aunt Kate and Sophia were very kind to the stranger. They stroked her fair hair and admired her dress, while greedy Otto ran away to hide the precious chain in a particular nook behind the beam, where he kept a bird-trap and fishing-rod. When supper was served, the dove child pecked daintily at the coarse bread, but she could not talk beyond making little cooing sounds quite like a dove.

"Aunt Katrine took off her star-spangled robe, and laid it away carefully for holidays; then she was dressed just like Sophia in a woollen petticoat and apron, yet she seemed a princess beside the honest little peasant lass; and you could have made nothing else of her, she was so delicate and pretty. The children both learned to love her after their own fashion. Otto considered that he owned her, and he scolded her as he did Sophia when she displeased him; yet he would not allow others to be rude to her, especially in the school, where all the village children met together.

"A long time passed, and the dove child appeared to have grown quite contented with her new life; she never tried to find the chain which Otto had concealed so cleverly. One day she paused in the meadow, and the other dove hovered down to alight on her hand. She received it with delight, cooing over it in her own tongue, just as if she had never learned another language.

"Otto found them talking together, and bade her catch the dove; but this she would not do, so the bird flew above the boy's reach.

"'If it comes again I will shoot it with a gun,' cried Otto, shaking his fist angrily.

"Then the dove child wept, and told her mate what the naughty boy had said; and the dove went away, not daring to return. The little girl begged Otto to restore her chain.

"'No, indeed,' said he. 'Your father must be a great king or prince from your appearance. When he comes to take you away in a gilded chariot drawn by splendid horses, he must give me ten chests of silver to make me rich. Then he may have you, and the chain also.'

"The dove child looked at him sadly.

"'You seem to care more for money already than your own good.'

"'I wish to have my own way,' cried Otto. 'Yes, and I will have it always!'

"She ran to Aunt Katrine, who always petted and soothed her, entreating her with many tears to find the chain which Otto had concealed so long ago.

"'What strange enchantment binds you, poor child?' asked the good woman, hoping to hear a story of magic. The stranger only shook her head sorrowfully, and looked away into the clear sky where the other dove had flown. After this she grew discontented and unhappy. Often would she watch for her mate, but the other never dared to appear, for fear Otto's bullet should pierce its tender breast.

"Aunt Katrine decided to find the chain, and release the child, whatever the result might be. She was an amiable old lady, and she rather dreaded Otto's ill-temper, so she asked him nothing about the matter, because she feared he would only hide the chain somewhere else. Besides, he was already growing to be a tall, stout lad, and would soon become master of the house. Accordingly, she chose an hour when the baking and sweeping were done for the day, the children away at school, and, putting on her spectacles, deliberately began the search.

"First she examined the chamber where Otto slept, but there she found nothing besides a few playthings. Then she remembered that the boy came down the ladder from the attic after he had run away with the chain on the day when the dove child was found; so up the creaking ladder went Aunt Katrine, and it was not long before she placed her hand directly on the chain as it lay coiled up snugly on the beam behind the bird-trap. She returned to the kitchen with the treasure, and, seating herself by the open window, admired the delicate chain, pol-

I

ishing the jewels on her sleeve the while, just to make them sparkle and glitter.

"A tiny black dwarf crept through the window like a spider, and perched on the back of Aunt Katrine's chair, without her being aware of his presence. The dwarf nodded and chuckled as he peered over her shoulder. After a while he drew a bit of folded paper from his girdle, which grew in size to a large fan, ornamented with strange figures and smelling of sweet perfume, and began gently to fan Aunt Katrine. The perfume was

thus wafted from the paper, and presently she bobbed her head twice, and sank back in the chair fast asleep. Oh, dear! she had done more harm than good with the best intentions. Down hopped the dwarf to the floor, and snatched the chain from her lap. She opened her heavy eyes just as he reached the door, where he took the chain in his mouth; then wings unfolded from his sides, and he flew away in the shape of the large black hawk which had first pursued the doves.

" There was no end of mischief done! Aunt Katrine wrung her hands over her folly in taking the chain from the safe hiding-place, and now some evil fairy had made off with it.

" The children were crossing the meadow at that moment.

" ' See the hawk up yonder with something in its mouth,' said Sophia.

" ' It must be a frog or a snake,' returned Otto, not dreaming that the precious chain was gone.

" Aunt Katrine said not a word, like the cowardly old body she was. What was the use? Otto would sulk for a month, and the dove child weep herself to death to think that she could never be restored to her own people, wherever they might be.

" Now the hawk was a wicked fairy, Skimp by name, who felt malice towards every one. When the fairy king's third wife died, leaving him an interesting widower, Skimp expected to be asked to marry him. Instead of that he chose her young maid-of-honor, and Skimp's temper was soured; so she went about in many shapes, not only tormenting the other fairies, but any chance mortal besides. In this way she made the acquaintance of all the giants and hobgoblins in the universe.

" ' Before I hide the chain where it cannot easily be found, I must do a trifle more mischief,' she thought, and paused near a great city where the smoke could be seen curling up from the chimneys, and the church spires were outnumbered by the masts of the shipping in the harbor. Here she changed her hawk dress to the costume of a country girl; a broad hat shaded a rosy, innocent face; she carried herself shyly and awkwardly; and no one could have believed that the simple lassie was shrewd, wicked Skimp, so perfect was her disguise.

"She entered a dingy building, where young men were busy counting money and writing in books. She wished to see their master the broker, and soon she was showing the wonderful chain, which she declared she desired to sell. Of course the broker wanted it; he would give his head for the diamond clasp alone; but he did not say so—oh no, he only shut one eye, and sighed that he could not offer more than two gold pieces for it—such a trifle! Skimp had been inside his brain, and whisked around twice to discover his thoughts, although she seemed to stand opposite all the while—a simple country girl.

"'I will take twenty gold pieces,' she said, firmly.

"The broker shook his head in horror; he would give four gold pieces, and no more. Then the fairy led the greedy broker a merry dance. Twice she gathered up the chain, and went out the door prepared to leave without completing the bargain, and twice the broker called her back, adding another coin to the pile on the counter. Finally he paid the full sum, pretending to shed tears at his own folly; and all the clerks paused with quills behind their ears to cry also, because their great employer did.

"Skimp departed with the money, leaving the broker delighted to have obtained the chain so cheaply.

"Fairies have no need of real money, so Skimp hid hers by the steps of a cathedral, where a good man found it and distributed the gold to the poor, which the broker would never have done.

" That night a large rat, with bright eyes like two beads, crept into the chamber where the broker slept. He had the chain in a stout oak box beneath the bed, and his door was barred, as he feared robbers. He could not keep out a rat, especially when that rat was Madam Skimp.

" She gnawed up a quantity of bank - notes to a soft pulp, which she had adroitly slipped from between the leaves of a pocket-book. With this she rolled two little balls, and popped them into the sleeper's ears, so that he could hear nothing. Then she attacked the box under the bed ; gnaw, gnaw, went her sharp teeth until a tiny hole was made, through which she dragged the dove chain, and away she went with it.

" ' That was well done,' said Skimp, changing into a hawk.

" We must now return to Aunt Katrine's house. The children all grew up. Sophia, a blooming maiden of eighteen, married a wealthy mill-owner, and went away.

" The dove child was tall and fair in appearance. She had long since outgrown the star-spangled robe and tiny shoes she first wore. The dove mate had never returned to visit her.

" Otto did not miss the chain from the hiding-place, for soon after Aunt Katrine had lost it the cottage caught fire from a smoking chimney, and the whole building was destroyed. Otto carried out the furniture, but he supposed the chain must have been lost in the flames. Aunt Katrine still kept silent, but she was very kind to the dove child, trying to repair the injury she had done her.

" ' After all, she is better off here in a Christian home,' thought poor Aunt Katrine, and then she looked at the spangled dress, wondering where the dove maiden really had lived.

"Otto had grown to be a handsome young man. He was faithful, industrious, and honest, and rebuilt the cottage with his own hands. Still he must always have his own way. He wished to marry the dove maiden. Aunt Katrine thought the girl could not do better—after she died there would be no one left to care for her unless she married Otto. So the dove maiden went into the new cottage as Otto's wife, although she wept many tears that this should be her lot instead of finding her dove companions once more. Aunt Katrine still scrubbed and polished, for in that lay her chief happiness, and the dove maiden was too delicate for such hard work. One fine morning the good aunt put on her spectacles to admire a pretty baby which lay in the cradle, as white as milk, with sapphire eyes. Otto made a good husband enough, and he was proud of his wife and child, but he was surly and ill-tempered if any little matter went wrong, even with them. The dove maiden

was now cheerful and happy; she called the child Snowdrop, and they gathered flowers together in the meadow, while Aunt Katrine scrubbed. When the little girl had grown sufficiently large she was dressed in the star-spangled robe, shoes, and silver cap which her mother had worn before her. Aunt Katrine was very much pleased with Snowdrop in this becoming costume. The dove maiden led her to the meadow, where she loved to sit near the spot where she had been captured. The Snyders had never heard a word of her story, but now she decided to tell it to Snowdrop, who listened with bright, intelligent eyes.

"'I dreamed about my sister last night,' she said. 'Perhaps if we wait patiently here she will come and pay us a visit.'

"'But how will she come?' asked Snowdrop.

"'She will fly here with her beautiful white wings, just as I did,' returned the dove maiden with a sigh. 'Attend, my child, while I tell you about your grandfather and relatives in the East. The King of Selgrobia is my father. He has a brilliant court thousands of miles away from here, where the palm-trees grow. I have a brother who is a Crown Prince, and will some time be king. My sister and I were the only daughters, and we were twins. We were born with little gold chains about our necks, studded with jewels, and clasped with a diamond button. These were gifts of the fairy king at our birth, and would enable us to become doves whenever we wished to fly away. The Queen, our mother, considered this a very dangerous gift; and, fearing we would avail ourselves of the chance thus granted us, she carefully hid the two chains away in a casket. We were brought up in the palace, yet seldom visited the state apartments. Ah, that was a happy life! We played in rose-gardens with our maids, and bathed in marble fountains.

"'One day there was a grand reception, in which a Prince of Ethiopia, black as ebony, and wearing a turban of yellow satin wound with chains of pearls, was presented to the King. The Crown Prince, our brother, was present at the ceremony; but we were too young, although our maids ran away to peep through the lattice at the wonderful stranger. Left alone, we rambled into our mother's magnificent apartments, and began to examine every rare, costly article of furniture with childish curiosity. Presently we found a casket in an alcove which contained our chains, and we at once recognized the fairy gifts.

"'" Let us go out on the balcony," urged my sister.

"'So we stepped out, disobeying our mother, and tried our wings as doves. We flew into the audience-hall, where the King sat in royal robes, and that was the last time I ever saw him. We sped up into the clear sky, and after a journey of many days reached this place. It is a cold region after my home.'

"As the mother ceased speaking, the dove sister came darting down to visit them. The dove maiden caressed the bird, shedding warm tears of joy upon its snowy feathers, and even Snowdrop stroked it with her fat little hands.

"'I have been to the fairy king,' said the dove. 'He says that the workman who made the chain is dead, and the art died with him, so we can never have another. The fairy sent this pearl ring to your daughter. No one can take it from her finger, and it will grant her wishes.'

"The mother and child returned to their humble home,

where Otto no sooner beheld the pearl ring than he tried to wrench it off; but the ring held as firmly as steel.

"'The value of the pearl would make me a rich man, and I will have it,' he scolded.

"The dove maiden was afraid he would hurt the child, and secretly made up her mind to send her away in search of her grandfather's kingdom. When Aunt Katrine saw the ring she was much excited, wishing to know where it came from; and little Snowdrop told her that a beautiful dove brought it from the skies. Then the old lady told the dove maiden the truth concerning the disappearance of the dove chain on the day when she had taken it from Otto's hiding-place under the eaves.

"'Never let him know,' she said, earnestly; and the dove maiden promised.

"'I will go and find the chain for you,' said Snowdrop to her mother. 'Then we can travel to the beautiful country you have told me about.'

"So the mother kissed Snowdrop; and the little girl, wearing the silver cap and the ring, started forth in search of the dove chain. She tripped along, humming a gay song to herself. She had left her dear mamma and Aunt Katrine looking sadly after her, yet she would soon return. A little robin flew on a twig, and sang—

"'Don't get into the boat.'

"'What do you say?' asked the child, puzzled.

"Then a toad hopped across the path, and croaked—

"'Don't get into the boat.'

"'I do not know what you are talking about,' laughed Snowdrop, and found herself on the brink of the canal. Directly before her was a boat, with gilded bows, the inside a soft pink-and-cream color, like the lining of a conch-shell, and the sail was like fine white silk. Of course, the little girl forgot the words croaked by the toad and sung by the robin, as warning, and stepped into the boat.

"'I will not move the anchor; I can just pretend to be sailing on the canal—that is all,' she said.

"A large white hand glided along under the boat, and slipped the chain which held it fastened to the shore. Snowdrop was

delighted; the boat slid along without the sail being hoisted. Had she but known it, two large white hands were pushing it steadily away from the bank.

"She enjoyed the sail, and she was also a trifle frightened, the current of the river seemed to be so very strong. A hawk came skimming close to the boat, holding a crystal bubble in its beak, which the bird dropped on Snowdrop's head. Crack went the bubble, scattering fine fragments all about, like diamond splinters, and a fragrant liquid flowed over the little girl's face. This bath made the young voyager feel exceedingly queer; she rubbed her eyelids wearily, her arms drooped, and she sank down into the bottom of the boat asleep.

"The hawk had a famous trick of putting people to sleep, as we have seen.

"The motion of the boat rocked her gently, like the softest

cradle, as she glided along more rapidly than ever. The two strong white hands pushed her past towns and hamlets straight onward; and if Snowdrop had been awake to peep over the side she would have seen not only the hands, but two fair arms, and a head covered with long, floating hair, like tangles of sea-weed.

" ' I have caught a pretty mouse—a new toy,' gurgled a soft voice down under the waves.

"When the little girl awoke and raised her head to gaze about her, there was wide, rolling sea extending from one side of the sky quite around to the other. The frail cockle-shell of a boat was tossed high in the air by the rough billows, and Snowdrop shrieked with terror every time she mounted a crest to plunge down the other side. Oh, how silly it was to get into the boat, and go to sleep! How she wished she was safe at home with her dear mamma and Aunt Katrine! She never once thought of her fairy ring, although it was on her finger all the time.

" A large wave towered high before the frightened child; the boat was upset, and she was caught in the white arms waiting to receive her, then borne swiftly and safely through the rush-ing waters.

" Before the bewildered traveller knew what she was about, she stood at the gates of a city. What surprised her most was the fact that her starry dress and silver cap were perfectly dry, although she was in the water all the while. This would not have been the case had not her fairy ring been on her finger.

" At first the city seemed to be precisely similar to cities on land: there were shops, squares, and palaces; and the wall was thickly crusted with oysters and barnacles, like a ship which has been in the water a long while. On closer inspection Snowdrop discovered the difference: the avenues were sand, the rows of buildings large shells. It would be easy to find the residence of a friend here if one was a stranger. There was a street composed wholly of cowries, another of clam-shells, another of scallops, a fourth of periwinkles, and so on, through all the kingdom of shells. Snowdrop was not surprised, therefore, to read on sign-boards—" Clam-shell Terrace," " Cowry Place," or " Periwinkle Avenue." She walked dry-shod through the streets, but she noticed that the inhabitants darted about swiftly and noiselessly, for they all had fish-tails. The city was very bright, almost as if illuminated with gas, and Snowdrop discovered that this light was shed from a sun-fish hung on a pole in a large park of sea-weeds. The sun-fish was phosphorescent, and at night the watchman was obliged to draw a blind over it, in order that the people should sleep a wink.

" In the centre of this sea-weed park was a building made of the bell of a jelly-fish, which was like the most beautiful crystal, or blown-glass, with pink-and-blue tints on the walls. Snowdrop could see people moving about inside this palace, and she approached it. Two sword-fish policemen hovered about the entrance.

" ' This is a prison,' they said, very fiercely.

" Snowdrop ran up the steps, and entered the first hall, where a group of mermaids were playing on coral harps with draped sea-lettuce. One of these took Snowdrop's hand—' I caught you, little maid, and I shall keep you for a pet.' The second

hall was spacious and beautiful; at the farther end was a throne
of rock, upon which sat a woman who was turned to stone, all
except her head, and bound with iron chains to her seat.

"Before her were open coffers and curious relics of all sorts,
with piles of silk fabrics, jewels, bars of gold, and coins, such as
are lost in shipwrecks.

"A number of young men and maidens, robed in dazzling
white, who were evidently her subjects, sorted the treasure into
chests; but the Queen did not seem to find any amusement
in their employment.

"Snowdrop approached, and was kindly received.

"'Have you seen my mother's dove chain?' asked the child.

"'I am Queen Kornor,' said the lady. 'This large city was
once located on a beautiful plain, surrounded by hills. The

Giant Drubb became angry with me because I neglected to invite him to a Christmas dinner, and he made an earthquake to sink us beneath the sea, while I was chained to the rock. Nothing but a blow from his iron dagger will release me.'

" ' I may be able to help you,' said Snowdrop.

" ' If you do, I will take you to a wise woman who lives on the mountain-side, and she must know all about the dove chain. The Giant Drubb lives on the borders of the Arabian Desert. Pause by the well under the palm-tree.'

" It was not easy to escape from the mermaid who had caught Snowdrop. She wished to present her to Neptune, she said, and she could not afford to lose her. Then Snowdrop clasped her arms about the neck of the lovely mermaid and kissed her, entreating that she might be released.

" ' I must find the dove chain for my mother, who is watching for me all this long time,' she pleaded; and the mermaid made not another word of objection, but carried her up to the shore. The mermaid was only frolicsome.

" How astonished the dove mother would have been to see her child carried in a mermaid's arms, with her star-robe crisp and dry!

" For the first time Snowdrop remembered to use her ring by wishing herself at the palm-tree, and she found herself there sooner than any steamboat could have taken her. She saw nobody, and looked down into the well. A rose-colored bubble came up to the surface from the cool depths.

" ' Don't pause to eat in the grove,' said a voice, and the bubble sank.

" Next a blue bubble appeared.

" ' Throw water over Drubb's heads,' and the second bubble sank.

" Then up came a green bubble.

" ' Carry the enchanted waters of this well.'

" ' What shall I carry it in ?'

" ' In me,' replied the green bubble, and popped out of the well upon the grass—a beautiful flask.

" Snowdrop walked through the grove, thinking she would soon finish the matter. Stately trees arched overhead to form a cool, green vault; the turf was velvet smooth, and along the paths were spread tempting fruits.

" Snowdrop recalled the words of the rosy bubble, and walked on, turning neither to the right nor left.

" Giant Drubb was seated in an immense arm-chair, hewn out of granite, which commanded a fine view of the surrounding country, so that he should know what was going on. Just as Snowdrop crept near, an ostrich ran in front of the giant and paused. Drubb stared at the ostrich with all the eyes in all his heads, because it was unusual to see an ostrich there.

" ' Come a step nearer, and I will catch you in my hand. You would make me a dainty breakfast,' cried Drubb.

" Snowdrop climbed behind him, and sprinkled his first two heads on the right with the enchanted water. This blinded his eyes; and always hiding behind the heads already sprinkled, she contrived to anoint the whole ten.

" ' Dear me !—is it night ?' growled Drubb. ' I thought the sun was still hours high. How short the days are growing !'

" Snowdrop slipped the dagger from its sheath at his side, and wished herself away from the terrible monster. The mer-

K

maid had waited for her on the shore, amusing herself by sing-
ing sweet songs to bewitch the fishermen.

" Down they went through the rushing waters, and this time
Snowdrop was not afraid. It was an easy matter to use
Drubb's dagger on the cruel chain which bound the lady, but
Snowdrop was surprised when the whole city rose to its place
on the blooming plain, the houses marble and stone, instead of
clam-shells and cowries.

" You see Giant Drubb had made a sort of off-hand earthquake to immerse the city; no one ever heard of a town
coming back that had been swallowed by a real, terrible earthquake. The Queen was very grateful. She lost no time in
leading Snowdrop up the steep path to the wise woman on
the mountain. They found her in a hut perched on a crag,
where a goat might climb — and, indeed, she was as nimble
and sure-footed as any goat. She liked to live near the stars,
where the thunder crashed and the lightning seemed to leap
from rock to rock.

" The visitors entered her hut, where an owl was perched on
one side of the hearth, and an eagle on the other.

" ' Who have we here ?' she muttered, peering at Snowdrop.

" ' I will give you my ring if you tell me where the dove
chain is,' said Snowdrop, eagerly.

" The wise woman smiled, and smoothed the little girl's hair.

" ' I live nearer the clear heavens than those below. The
stars are my jewels,' she said.

" ' This dear child has rescued me from prison, and in return she desires to find her mother's dove chain,' said Queen
Kornor.

" ' Yes, yes—I know. Madam Skimp did all that mischief because she could not marry the fairy king; and it was his gift. I hear all the news from my two friends here.'

" ' I saw Skimp fly away with the chain in the form of a hawk,' said the eagle.

" The wise woman sprinkled some dried herbs on a brazier, and a white cloud rose in the hut, so that the two visitors could not see her at all. When the smoke cleared, she shook her head.

" ' Go to the fairy king. Perhaps Skimp will tell you, after all.'

" The eagle offered to carry the guests down the mountain on his back, and they found the ride very pleasant. Snowdrop could only think of her lonely mother now, who must watch anxiously for her return, and so decided to seek the fairy realm at once.

" Everything was in confusion ; the fairy queen had been stung by a gnat, which caused her death, and the king was again a widower.

" ' That comes of marrying beneath his rank. She was only Skimp's maid of honor,' cried the gossips.

" Snowdrop heard them, for she stood behind the bluebell in which they were swinging.

" ' Bless me !' exclaimed one, raising her eye-glass, which was made of the eye-hole of a cambric needle set in steel; ' who comes here ?   It is Madam Skimp, and no other !'

" Sure enough, it was Skimp, who had heard of the queen's death, and decided to return to the court, in hopes of winning the seat on the throne beside the king.

" Skimp was lovely.   She had bathed her face in flower-dew; her robe was sewed out of gold leaf, with a boddice formed of a single ruby, and trimmed with diamond dust. Her hair was combed into a high waterfall; her hat was made of a beetle, and her fan was dandelion down. Never was a more charming toilet seen; the other fairy ladies nearly died of envy when she minced along, waving her fan in a fashionable manner; and in kneeling before the king she showed two little gold boots, with red heels, to great advantage.

" The king thought he had never seen Skimp look so pretty; and when he bade her rise from her knees, he proposed to drink her health in amber honey, which was served in beech-nut cups. Although he was still dressed in mourning (a sable moth's cloak), as a token of respect for the departed queen, he had not sipped all of the honey before he made Skimp an offer of marriage.

" The honey sweetened her temper wonderfully—that or prosperity—and she began to feel ashamed of her naughtiness.

" Snowdrop made her presence known, for the little people were so much absorbed in their own affairs that they had not noticed her.

" The king invited her to be seated on the soft moss, as his chair was too small for a mortal; and you have no idea how big and clumsy she appeared among the Fairies, quite as great a contrast as Giant Drubb was to herself.

" ' Dear, good Fairies, I have been all over the earth to find my mother's dove chain, and I need your assistance.'

" ' I should be ashamed of my subjects if they did not help you,' replied the king. ' Every fairykin must hold up a hand in token of willingness to aid Snowdrop.'

" Each one held up a tiny fist, and Queen Skimp raised hers with the rest. Why not? She was willing to restore the chain since she had been sweetened with the honey.

" ' Let by-gones be by-gones,' she said. ' If I was not the fourth wife, I am the fifth.'

" She flew away on her gauze wings, and returned in a trice, carrying the chain, which she gave to Snowdrop, and kissed her in the bargain.

" Snowdrop left the Fairies in the midst of wedding gayeties, thankful that Skimp's ambition had been at last gratified, since this had led her to give up the chain, as well as to become a good sprite at last.

" Danger was not over for the dove mother's little daughter. Scarcely had she quitted the fairy kingdom when she heard behind her a rumbling like distant thunder. This sound was caused by Giant Drubb, who was tramping after the bold girl who had robbed him of his iron dagger to release Queen Kornor from her enchantment under the sea.

"Snowdrop, with the aid of her ring, changed herself into a lily, which held the chain in its cup securely, and the giant strode on without noticing the flower trembling on its stalk. Afterwards she resumed her journey, and walked behind the giant, keeping out of range of his many eyes, that looked in all directions.

"When Snowdrop reached the canal and the meadow, Giant Drubb was still striding forward, looking before him, like a great many other big people; and perhaps he is still marching around the world, for Snowdrop saw him no more.

"How quickly she ran across the meadow to the village! How gladly the dove mother and Aunt Katrine welcomed her! Otto was still cross over Snowdrop's long absence, of whom he was fond in his way.

"Next morning he went to his labor in the fields, and Aunt Katrine stood all the copper pots of the kitchen in a row to be freshly scoured. At that moment Snowdrop pulled her mother gently away through the door. Hastily throwing the chain around the dove mother's neck, she wished to become a carrier-pigeon at the same moment, and they rose in the air together.

"Otto was binding sheaves, and did not notice that two birds hovered overhead. A ring fell before him, and he discovered a pile of gold. He missed wife and child, but the pile of gold remained.

"They then flew towards the sun and their kindred.

"Aunt Katrine and the village people thought that they were dead, and had gone to heaven."

Queen Puff was in high good-humor with herself and the rest of the company when she had finished her story.

"It comes from the Old Country, and is all the better for that, to my fancy. Let me hear what your Indian and Yankee Fairies have to say after the 'Dove Maiden.'"

"Hoighty-toighty! I could make up a better story with my eyes shut," retorted Nip.

Then Queen Puff grew quite red in the face, and was about to reply, when the attention of all was diverted.

In Job's picture-gallery there was a small print of an oasis in the desert, where one slender palm-tree towered aloft, shading the well which afforded refreshment to a company of Arabs and camels. This palm-tree began to rustle and sway gently, as if disturbed by a breeze, as indeed it was—the breeze of Nip's influence.

"A great deal has been said about America this evening," said the tree. "Let me describe how the first cocoa-nut was discovered.

THE FIRST COCOA-NUT.

" A PRINCE once lived in the East, who fell ill, just like the poorest of his subjects. The Prince in those countries was called a Rajah, which means much the same thing. There was no help for it; disease had entered the Rajah's house of stucco, with the teak-wood balconies, as if he were a humble laborer, living in a hut, and eating a handful of rice a day.

" What was the matter with him ? Nobody knew, and wise doctors came miles and miles to consult over the mysterious malady and discover a remedy, but all to no purpose. The wise doctors, as well as all the subjects, believed that Maha-Laka, a great demon, had thus afflicted the Rajah because he was a good man.

" There was really nothing more to be done, since the physicians were at their wits' end.

" The Rajah did not forget to say his prayers, however great his sufferings; so he went to the temple, offered a whole pyramid of sweet flowers on the altar, according to the formula of the Buddhist religion, and repeated the Buddha-Sarana.

" Then he came home to the teak-wood palace, laid down on his mat, and slept for seven days. Slaves hovered about him, burning perfumes in braziers, and waving fans of peacock feathers to cool the chamber, yet none dared to disturb his slumbers.

" The Rajah was dreaming a wonderful dream all this while. He saw a beach, and water beyond. Waves broke on the strand, and a thousand dazzling lights shifted over the sparkling blue surface. It seemed a curious fact that when the Rajah dipped his hand into the clear, cool-looking water to drink, the flavor was salt and disagreeable.

" Gazing around on the strange scene, he discovered a grove of trees, rooted on the very brink where land and water met —the spray dashed over their trunks. These trees rose in slender columns, like mine, with a crown of graceful foliage at the top. Yes, it was wonderful ! While the Rajah marvelled, a cobra-de-capello, the snake sacred to the Buddhists, glided to his side, raised its spectacled hood, thrust out its blue, forked tongue, bowed its head three times, and lapped water from the leaf reserved for the Prince's private use. Then the cobra disappeared in the jungle. This was proof enough of Buddha's favor.

" A cloud gathered close about him, which the Prince tried in vain to pierce, growing darker and darker until it was night. He was afraid of this cloud, and fixed his eyes anxiously on a rift which clove the vapor like sunshine. Out of this splendor grew an old man, whose face was calm, like the moon, and he sat on the mist with his feet crossed. The Rajah knew that this must be Maha-Sarana, the father of Buddha; so he fell on his face, pressing his forehead to the ground in the way his own subjects did when approaching him.

" ' This is a sacred tree,' said the old man, pointing to the grove by the sea. ' You have failed, through ignorance, to show it the respect due to all created things. See ! The deeply serrated leaf distinguishes it as the favorite of Buddha. The snake was kind to Buddha while he was on earth, and therefore, since the cobra has drank from your leaf, you shall recover health by obeying my commands.

" 'In the South lies your remedy. A journey of one hundred hours will bring you to the trees seen by you in this vision. Eat of the fruit, which must be your sole diet until the Great Moon has twice given and refused her light. Disease shall leave thee, but forget not sweet sacrifice to that Brahma of all Brahmas to whom even demons pay homage. The fruit, which is partly a transparent fluid and partly innocent food, grows on the top; by fire alone can it be obtained.'

" A sound as of a thousand tomtoms broke on the Rajah's ear, and he awoke.

" The pious Prince at once arose, placed the palms of his hands on his forehead, and bowed himself in prayer to Ossah Pollah Dewyo, the ruler and creator of all gods and demons, and of the flat earth besides.

" Next an offering of fruits, betel-leaves, and flowers was left under a Bogaha-tree; and it was proclaimed that the invalid would make a journey.

" Forth came the retinue of warriors and slaves—forth came the wife from her zenana, wrapped in shawls and veiled with gauze, through which twinkled the jewels of a princess, attended by troops of dancing-girls and waiting-women.

" The Rajah climbed a silver ladder to the velvet howdah on the elephant's back; the Princess was seated in her litter of ivory and fragrant woods, and the royal procession moved in obedience to the command of the old man seen in the dream.

" Through rivers, forests, valleys, and the tangled jungle our Rajah made his way to the South.

" At last he saw the wide expanse of sea, the blue waters; and on the margin the trees with slender pillars of trunk and feathered crown. This crest served as a parasol to shade the fruit from the vertical rays of the sun, and directly beneath hung the purple and yellow clusters. No human being lived on this wild shore; only leopards, elephants, lions, and sloths roamed about. Who could climb the tree? No one, surely. The Rajah had a fire built; flames girdled and sapped its life with intense heat, until the crown trembled, wavered, and fell. Out ran innumerable creatures that had found a home in its branches — large blue scorpions, brown centipedes, black and green beetles, tarantulas, the polonga, and rat-snake.

" Descending from the elephant, the Rajah approached the

beach, and tasted the water. It was salt and bitter to the palate, like it had been in his dream.

" The first cocoa-nut was broken, and forth gushed the milk, as pure and deliciously cool as crystal. The Rajah's life was saved by this food.

" In his gratitude he made known to all the world that he had discovered a tree the fruit of which was renewed health, the leaf adapted to making huts, mats, fans, and thread, the sap a refreshing liquor, and the pith a nutritious meal."

In the picture the Arabs watered their camels, and prepared to cross the desert ; but they got no farther in their movements, because they were taken in those attitudes.

" I can't make out all that you say," Job remarked, looking at the palm-tree. " Who was Buddha ?"

" If you have heard of the heathen you know what I mean. The Rajah was a heathen, and worshipped the god Buddha, as a great many people do in the East. The missionaries go to those lands to teach them better, and tell them about Christ."

Then the palm-tree became part of the picture again.

The tiny visitors grew restless ; as for Nip he appeared and disappeared continually, now climbing among the old blue ware of the open cupboard, now dancing on Grandfather's spectacle-case, now seating himself in the steel thimble on the shelf as if it were a tub. However, Job and the Fairies did not expect Nip to behave well. The Angora cat gave a leap in the air, and came down with her fur standing on end.

" It must be time for the Fairy of the Cascade," she purred.

" Bang ! bang !" went the old clock, as if in answer.

Then it seemed to Job that the kitchen wall melted away, and he saw the fall, framed in the ravine, with the hollowed space below where he had crept many a time to catch the spray. The banks were crusted with snow, dazzling and pure; every tree and shrub sparkled with frozen drops; and the water did not leap over the crag as in summer, but formed a sheet of ice, as if Nature had fashioned out of the rocks a great organ, and these were pipes for the winds to play.

Two hands linked together by an ice chain opened the doors of the cascade—it seemed the most ordinary thing possible to Job just then—and he looked into the recesses of the hills. There sat the lovely Fairy of the Cascade bewailing her imprisonment by cruel Winter.

" He says it does me good, and makes me value my freedom in the spring all the more," she moaned. " How I love the sun for coming to release me! At present he is busy in other parts of the world, you know. Winter is the most suspicious tyrant. He would not allow me to visit you with the other Fairies, because he did not trust me that I would not run away and make myself a new channel in some other ravine."

Job longed to ask for his present, but was too shy.

Then a little voice behind him — it sounded like Nip's — inquired :

" Where is Job's Christmas gift?"

The Fairy looked kindly at the boy.

" My gift is the magic pole, to help one leap ravines and over the largest rocks. I shall save it for some other child, now, because you already own it."

"Oh, no I don't—not even a stick," protested Job.

"My dear Job, the magic pole is cheerfulness, which helps mortals to jump over trials and sorrows, forgetting their own selfish pleasure. This you already own."

Job was puzzled beyond measure. The chained hands closed the ice door of the cascade, and the wall of the kitchen was in its proper place.

"Bless me! The children will not get their dream-thread in time," said Puff, bustling about.

"A merry Christmas to you, Job," piped all the little voices.

The Summer Fairies mingled with winter's frosty elves; Puff and the Laurel Sprites rose in a brilliant cloud. It made Job giddy to watch them—red and green and pink in circles like a dissolving rainbow—until he shut his eyes tight to escape the dazzling radiance. Hark! Who called?

Job was sitting in Grandfather's chair, which was drawn up to the hearth, where the log still flickered; and the friendly sun was not only peeping in the window, but streaming across his face. Evidently it was day—Christmas-day. Where were Nip and Queen Puff? Gone.

The Angora cat stood at Job's feet, staring at him with all her eyes; the shell lay on the shelf, the clock ticked in its corner.

Job roused himself, and went to the window. Snow had ceased to fall; the sky was blue and clear. He raised the sash. Outside a white field stretched almost unbroken by line of fence or bush; the flakes had fallen all night.

"Holloa!" came the sound again, echoed by all the hills.

Job's heart began to beat hard. They were calling him! Was he to be dug out of the drift safely? He put his hands to his mouth, shaped them like a trumpet, and sent a cheery shout ringing back. Then he danced around the kitchen; and, because he must do something in his joy at hearing voices again, he snatched up the cat, and hugged her until pussy yelled aloud with wrath.

How about the poor cow and the chickens? Job strove to trace the path he had made with so much labor the day before, but the snow had covered it. The cow must wait longer for her breakfast than on the previous day. In the meanwhile Job was a hero without knowing it. The night before news had spread from the village to farm after farm that the boy was alone on the mountain, and when the snow ceased all were ready to turn out with sleighs and ploughs to force a way through to rescue him.

Grandfather could neither sleep nor eat for thinking of what evil might have befallen Job in his absence. Perhaps he had left the shelter of his home to seek help at some distant house, and had perished in the storm! The old man's fears grew with the drifts, as it were. Many hands make light work; the farmers toiled with a will, and cheered up Grandfather. They found an unexpected ally where the task seemed most difficult. The still cold which nipped Job's toes as the fire went down performed for him a better service—it froze the crust of the snow so that a sleigh could pass over it. This was the party whose call Job heard.

There never was a boy quite so glad to see faces again as Job was, and to have Grandfather among them too. All the farmers laughed as if it were a great joke, and shook Job by the shoulders; that was their way of expressing satisfaction. Grandfather felt of the boy carefully to judge if he were frost-bitten or hurt; then he sank down into his chair, and exclaimed:

" Wal, this never happened to us afore !"

You may be sure that the cow and the chickens were reached in a trice, with all those strong arms to clear the way; and by the time that was done the tea-kettle sang merrily, the table was spread, and Grandfather was engaged in making some of his famous pancakes. The neighbors stayed for a while, and the Angora cat felt herself quite in the shade with so many visitors.

Job stood at the window when the sky had assumed the

L.

green tinge of a cold twilight. He was thinking of his fairy visitors, and wishing that they would return.

The Lady of the Cascade was in her winter prison—one knew exactly where to find her; but roguish Nip and busy Puff, with her endless spinning, were gone.

" The Fairies came to see me last night—because I was lonely, I guess," said the boy, gravely. " They told me, oh, such wonderful things, if I could remember 'em all."

Grandfather looked at Job over the rim of his spectacles. To tell the truth, he was afraid that his grandson was a little cracked.

" There was Nip from the Berkshire Hills, and the Indian Fairies who live here still—they told about the witch child, and—"

" Pooh !" interrupted Grandfather, looking down again at the open pocket-book where lay the money he had brought. " You were asleep and dreamed it."

Job was so astonished and indignant that he could not utter one word. What did Grandfather know about it? Perhaps the shell and the cat had not talked! He would be saying that next.

After Grandfather had gone to bed, our hero stole into the kitchen to see if there were an elfish company gathered around the hearth. No, the fire blazed and flickered, and had the chimney all to itself. That was all.

" You know about the Fairies, don't you?" Job whispered to the old clock.

" Tick, tick, tick !" said the clock, which might mean anything, or just nothing at all.

" Pussy, what did Nip say ?"

The Angora cat lay curled in a white ball on the chair.

" Miouw !" she answered, blinking stupidly.

Job crept away slowly. Was Grandfather right, after all, when he said it was a dream ?

This is our story. If any little boy or girl who visits the Catskills next summer will look for Job, not many miles from the Mountain House, he may be found, shy and barefooted, wearing the jacket made out of Grandfather's old plum-colored coat. If he should not be recognized by this description, the chances are ten to one that the Angora cat will be close be-side him.

VALUABLE & INTERESTING WORKS

FOR PUBLIC AND PRIVATE LIBRARIES,

Published by HARPER & BROTHERS, New York.

MOTLEY'S DUTCH REPUBLIC. The Rise of the Dutch Republic. A History. By JOHN LOTHROP MOTLEY, LL.D., D.C.L. With a Portrait of William of Orange. 3 vols., 8vo, Cloth, $10 50; Sheep, $12 00; Half Calf, Extra, $17 25.

MOTLEY'S UNITED NETHERLANDS. History of the United Netherlands: from the Death of William the Silent to the Twelve Years' Truce. With a full View of the English-Dutch Struggle against Spain, and of the Origin and Destruction of the Spanish Armada. By JOHN LOTHROP MOTLEY, LL.D., D.C.L. Portraits. 4 vols., 8vo, Cloth, $14 00; Sheep, $16 00; Half Calf, Extra, $23 00.

MOTLEY'S LIFE AND DEATH OF JOHN OF BARNEVELD. Life and Death of John of Barneveld, Advocate of Holland. With a View of the Primary Causes and Movements of "The Thirty-Years' War." By JOHN LOTHROP MOTLEY, D.C.L. With Illustrations. 2 vols., 8vo, Cloth, $7 00; Sheep, $8 00; Half Calf, $11 50.

TRISTRAM'S LAND OF MOAB. The Land of Moab: The Result of Travels and Discoveries on the East Side of the Dead Sea and the Jordan. By H. B. TRISTRAM, M.A., LL.D., F.R.S. With a Chapter on the Persian Palace of Mashita, by JAS. FERGUSON, F.R.S. With Maps and Ill's. Crown 8vo, Cloth, $2 50.

SCHWEINFURTH'S HEART OF AFRICA. The Heart of Africa; or, Three Years' Travels and Adventures in the Unexplored Regions of the Centre of Africa. From 1868 to 1871. By Dr. GEORG SCHWEINFURTH. Translated by ELLEN E. FREWER. With an Introduction by WINWOOD READE. Illustrated by about 130 Woodcuts from Drawings made by the Author, and with two Maps. 2 vols., 8vo, Cloth, $8 00.

FLAMMARION'S ATMOSPHERE. The Atmosphere. Translated from the French of CAMILLE FLAMMARION. Edited by JAMES GLAISHER, F.R.S., Superintendent of the Magnetical and Meteorological Department of the Royal Observatory at Greenwich. With 10 Chromo-Lithographs and 86 Woodcuts. 8vo, Cloth, $6 00.

EVANGELICAL ALLIANCE CONFERENCE, 1873. History, Essays, Orations, and Other Documents of the Sixth General Conference of the Evangelical Alliance, held in New York Oct. 2-12, 1873. Edited by Rev. PHILIP SCHAFF, D.D., and Rev. S. IRENÆUS PRIME, D.D. With Portraits of Rev. Messrs. Pronier, Carrasco, and Cook, recently deceased. 8vo, Cloth, nearly 800 pages, $6 00.

SANTO DOMINGO, Past and Present: with a Glance at Hayti. By SAMUEL HAZARD. Maps and Illustrations. Crown 8vo, Cloth, $3 50.

BALDWIN'S PRE-HISTORIC NATIONS. Pre-Historic Nations; or, Inquiries concerning some of the Great Peoples and Civilizations of Antiquity, and their Probable Relation to a still Older Civilization of the Ethiopians or Cushites of Arabia. By JOHN D. BALDWIN, Member of the American Oriental Society. 12mo, Cloth, $1 75.

DRAKE'S NOOKS AND CORNERS OF THE NEW ENGLAND COAST. Nooks and Corners of the New England Coast. By SAMUEL ADAMS DRAKE, Author of "Old Landmarks of Boston," "Historic Fields and Mansions of Middlesex," &c. With numerous Illustrations. 8vo, Cloth, $3 50.

GREEN'S SHORT HISTORY OF THE ENGLISH PEOPLE. A Short History of the English People. By J. R. GREEN, M.A., Examiner in the School of Modern History, Oxford. With Tables and Colored Maps. 8vo, Cloth, $1 75.

MOHAMMED AND MOHAMMEDANISM: Lectures Delivered at the Royal Institution of Great Britain in February and March, 1874. By R. BOSWORTH SMITH, M.A., Assistant Master in Harrow School; late Fellow of Trinity College, Oxford. With an Appendix containing Emanuel Deutsch's Article on "Islam." 12mo, Cloth, $1 50.

POETS OF THE NINETEENTH CENTURY. The Poets of the Nineteenth Century. Selected and Edited by the Rev. ROBERT ARIS WILLMOTT. With English and American Additions, arranged by EVERT A. DUYCKINCK, Editor of "Cyclopædia of American Literature." Comprising Selections from the Greatest Authors of the Age. Superbly Illustrated with 141 Engravings from Designs by the most Eminent Artists. New and Enlarged Edition. In elegant Square 8vo form, printed on Superfine Tinted Paper, richly bound in extra Cloth, Beveled, Gilt Edges, $5 00; Half Calf, $5 50; Full Turkey Morocco, $9 00.

THE REVISION OF THE ENGLISH VERSION OF THE NEW TESTAMENT. By LIGHTFOOT, TRENCH, and ELLICOTT. With an Introduction by the Rev. P. SCHAFF, D.D. 618 pp., Crown 8vo, Cloth, $3 00. This work embraces in one volume:

I. ON A FRESH REVISION OF THE ENGLISH NEW TESTAMENT. By J. B. LIGHTFOOT, D.D., Canon of St. Paul's, and Hulsean Professor of Divinity, Cambridge. Second Edition, Revised. 196 pp.

II. ON THE AUTHORIZED VERSION OF THE NEW TESTAMENT in Connection with some Recent Proposals for its Revision. By RICHARD CHENEVIX TRENCH, D.D., Archbishop of Dublin. 194 pp.

III. CONSIDERATIONS ON THE REVISION OF THE ENGLISH VERSION OF THE NEW TESTAMENT. By J. C. ELLICOTT, D.D., Bishop of Gloucester and Bristol. 178 pp.

ADDISON'S COMPLETE WORKS. The Works of Joseph Addison, embracing the whole of the "Spectator." Complete in 3 vols., 8vo, Cloth, $6 00.

SIR SAMUEL BAKER'S ISMAILÏA. Ismailïa: A Narrative of the Expedition to Central Africa for the Suppression of the Slave Trade. Organized by ISMAIL, Khedive of Egypt. By Sir SAMUEL W. BAKER, Pasha, M.A., F.R.S., F.R.G.S. With Maps, Portraits, and upward of Fifty full-page Illustrations by ZWECKER and DURAND. 8vo, Cloth, $5 00.

NORDHOFF'S CALIFORNIA. California: for Health, Pleasure, and Residence. A Book for Travellers and Settlers. By CHARLES NORDHOFF. With Illustrations. 8vo, Cloth, $2 50.

NORDHOFF'S NORTHERN CALIFORNIA, OREGON, AND THE SANDWICH ISLANDS. Northern California, Oregon, and the Sandwich Islands. By CHARLES NORDHOFF. Profusely Illustrated. 8vo, Cloth, $2 50.

NORDHOFF'S COMMUNISTIC SOCIETIES OF THE UNITED STATES. The Communistic Societies of the United States; from Personal Visit and Observation: including Detailed Accounts of the Economists, Zoarites, Shakers, the Amana, Oneida, Bethel, Aurora, Icarian, and Other Existing Societies, their Religious Creeds, Social Practices, Numbers, Industries, and Present Condition. By CHARLES NORDHOFF. With Illustrations. 8vo, Cloth, $4 00.

VINCENT'S LAND OF THE WHITE ELEPHANT. The Land of the White Elephant. Sights and Scenes in Southeastern Asia. A Personal Narrative of Travel and Adventure in Farther India, embracing the Countries of Burma, Siam, Cambodia, and Cochin-China (1871-2). By FRANK VINCENT, Jr. With Map, Plans, and numerous Illustrations. Crown 8vo, Cloth, $3 50.

MYERS'S REMAINS OF LOST EMPIRES. Remains of Lost Empires. Sketches of the Ruins of Palmyra, Nineveh, Babylon, and Persepolis, with some Notes on India and the Cashmerian Himalayas. By P. V. N. MYERS, A.M. Illustrations. 8vo, Cloth, $3 50.

HAYDN'S DICTIONARY OF DATES, relating to all Ages and Nations. For Universal Reference. Edited by BENJAMIN VINCENT, Assistant Secretary and Keeper of the Library of the Royal Institution of Great Britain; and Revised for the Use of American Readers. 8vo, Cloth, $5 00; Sheep, $6 00.

MACGREGOR'S ROB ROY ON THE JORDAN. The Rob Roy on the Jordan, Nile, Red Sea, and Gennesareth, &c. A Canoe Cruise in Palestine and Egypt, and the Waters of Damascus. By J. MACGREGOR, M.A. With Maps and Illustrations. Crown 8vo, Cloth, $2 50.

WALLACE'S MALAY ARCHIPELAGO. The Malay Archipelago: the Land of the Orang-Utan, and the Bird of Paradise. A Narrative of Travel, 1854-'62. With Studies of Man and Nature. By ALFRED RUSSEL WALLACE. With Maps and numerous Illustrations. Crown 8vo, Cloth, $2 50.

WHYMPER'S ALASKA. Travel and Adventure in the Territory of Alaska, formerly Russian America —now Ceded to the United States—and in various other Parts of the North Pacific. By FREDERICK WHYMPER. With Map and Illustrations. Crown 8vo, Cloth, $2 50.

ORTON'S ANDES AND THE AMAZON. The Andes and the Amazon: or, Across the Continent of South America. By JAMES ORTON, M.A., Professor of Natural History in Vassar College, Poughkeepsie, N. Y., and Corresponding Member of the Academy of Natural Sciences, Philadelphia. With a New Map of Equatorial America and numerous Illustrations. Crown 8vo, Cloth, $2 00.

WINCHELL'S SKETCHES OF CREATION. Sketches of Creation: a Popular View of some of the Grand Conclusions of the Sciences in reference to the History of Matter and of Life. Together with a Statement of the Intimations of Science respecting the Primordial Condition and the Ultimate Destiny of the Earth and the Solar System. By ALEXANDER WINCHELL, LL.D. With Illustrations. 12mo, Cloth, $2 00.

WHITE'S MASSACRE OF ST. BARTHOLOMEW. The Massacre of St. Bartholomew: Preceded by a History of the Religious Wars in the Reign of Charles IX. By HENRY WHITE, M.A. With Illustrations. 8vo, Cloth, $1 75.

LOSSING'S FIELD-BOOK OF THE REVOLUTION. Pictorial Field-Book of the Revolution; or, Illustrations by Pen and Pencil of the History, Biography, Scenery, Relics, and Traditions of the War for Independence. By BENSON J. LOSSING. 2 vols., 8vo, Cloth, $14 00; Sheep, $15 00; Half Calf, $18 00; Full Turkey Morocco, Gilt Edges, $22 00.

LOSSING'S FIELD-BOOK OF THE WAR OF 1812. Pictorial Field-Book of the War of 1812; or, Illustrations by Pen and Pencil of the History, Biography, Scenery, Relics, and Traditions of the last War for American Independence. By BENSON J. LOSSING. With 882 Illustrations, engraved on Wood by Lossing & Barritt, chiefly from Original Sketches by the Author. Complete in One Volume, 1084 pages, large 8vo. Price, in Cloth, $7 00; Sheep, $8 50; Full Roan, $9 00; Half Calf or Half Morocco extra, $10 00; Full Morocco, Gilt Edges, $12 00.

ALFORD'S GREEK TESTAMENT. The Greek Testament: with a critically revised Text; a Digest of Various Readings; Marginal References to Verbal and Idiomatic Usage; Prolegomena; and a Critical and Exegetical Commentary. For the Use of Theological Students and Ministers. By HENRY ALFORD, D.D., Dean of Canterbury. Vol. I., containing the Four Gospels. 944 pages, 8vo, Cloth, $6 00; Sheep, $6 50.

ABBOTT'S FREDERICK THE GREAT. The History of Frederick the Second, called Frederick the Great. By JOHN S. C. ABBOTT. Elegantly Illustrated. 8vo, Cloth, $5 00.

ABBOTT'S HISTORY OF THE FRENCH REVOLUTION. The French Revolution of 1789, as viewed in the Light of Republican Institutions. By JOHN S. C. ABBOTT. With 100 Engravings. 8vo, Cloth, $5 00.

ABBOTT'S NAPOLEON BONAPARTE. The History of Napoleon Bonaparte. By JOHN S. C. ABBOTT. With Maps, Woodcuts, and Portraits on Steel. 2 vols., 8vo, Cloth, $10 00.

ABBOTT'S NAPOLEON AT ST. HELENA; or, Interesting Anecdotes and Remarkable Conversations of the Emperor during the Five and a Half Years of his Captivity. Collected from the Memorials of Las Casas, O'Meara, Montholon, Antommarchi, and others. By JOHN S. C. ABBOTT. With Illustrations. 8vo, Cloth, $5 00.

ALCOCK'S JAPAN. The Capital of the Tycoon: a Narrative of a Three Years' Residence in Japan. By Sir RUTHERFORD ALCOCK, K.C.B., Her Majesty's Envoy Extraordinary and Minister Plenipotentiary in Japan. With Maps and Engravings. 2 vols., 12mo, Cloth, $3 50.

ALISON'S HISTORY OF EUROPE. FIRST SERIES: From the Commencement of the French Revolution, in 1789, to the Restoration of the Bourbons, in 1815. [In addition to the Notes on Chapter LXXVI., which correct the errors of the original work concerning the United States, a copious Analytical Index has been appended to this American edition.] SECOND SERIES: From the Fall of Napoleon, in 1815, to the Accession of Louis Napoleon, in 1852. 8 vols., 8vo, Cloth, $16 00.

BARTH'S NORTH AND CENTRAL AFRICA. Travels and Discoveries in North and Central Africa. Being a Journal of an Expedition undertaken under the Auspices of H.B.M.'s Government in the Years 1849-1855. By HENRY BARTH, Ph.D., D.C.L. Illustrated. 3 vols., 8vo, Cloth, $12 00.

BRODHEAD'S HISTORY OF NEW YORK. History of the State of New York. By JOHN ROMEYN BRODHEAD. 1609-1691. Two Vols. 8vo, Cloth, $3 00 per vol.

BOSWELL'S JOHNSON. The Life of Samuel Johnson, LL.D. Including a Journey to the Hebrides. By JAMES BOSWELL, Esq. A New Edition, with numerous Additions and Notes. By JOHN WILSON CROKER, LL.D., F.R.S. Portrait of Boswell. 2 vols., 8vo, Cloth, $4 00.

HENRY WARD BEECHER'S SERMONS. Sermons by HENRY WARD BEECHER, Plymouth Church, Brooklyn. Selected from Published and Unpublished Discourses, and Revised by their Author. With Steel Portrait. Complete in 2 vols., 8vo, Cloth, $5 00.

LYMAN BEECHER'S AUTOBIOGRAPHY, &c. Autobiography, Correspondence, &c., of Lyman Beecher, D.D. Edited by his Son, CHARLES BEECHER. With Three Steel Portraits and Engravings on Wood. 2 vols., 12mo, Cloth, $5 00.

DRAPER'S CIVIL WAR. History of the American Civil War. By JOHN W. DRAPER, M.D., LL.D., Professor of Chemistry and Physiology in the University of New York. In Three Vols. 8vo, Cloth, $3 50 per vol.

DRAPER'S INTELLECTUAL DEVELOPMENT OF EUROPE. A History of the Intellectual Development of Europe. By JOHN W. DRAPER, M.D., LL.D., Professor of Chemistry and Physiology in the University of New York. 8vo, Cloth, $5 00.

DRAPER'S AMERICAN CIVIL POLICY. Thoughts on the Future Civil Policy of America. By JOHN W. DRAPER, M.D., LL.D., Professor of Chemistry and Physiology in the University of New York. Crown 8vo, Cloth, $2 50.

DU CHAILLU'S AFRICA. Explorations and Adventures in Equatorial Africa; with Accounts of the Manners and Customs of the People, and of the Chase of the Gorilla, the Crocodile, Leopard, Elephant, Hippopotamus, and other Animals. By PAUL B. DU CHAILLU. Numerous Illustrations. 8vo, Cloth, $5 00.

DU CHAILLU'S ASHANGO LAND. A Journey to Ashango Land, and Further Penetration into Equatorial Africa. By PAUL B. DU CHAILLU. New Edition. Handsomely Illustrated. 8vo, Cloth, $5 00.

BROUGHAM'S AUTOBIOGRAPHY. Life and Times of HENRY, LORD BROUGHAM. Written by Himself. In Three Volumes. 12mo, Cloth, $2 00 per vol.

BULWER'S ESSAYS. Miscellaneous Prose Works of Edward Bulwer, Lord Lytton, including "Caxtoniana." 3 vols., 12mo, Cloth, $5 25.

BULWER'S HORACE. The Odes and Epodes of Horace. A Metrical Translation into English. With Introduction and Commentaries. By LORD LYTTON. With Latin Text from the Editions of Orelli, Macleane, and Yonge. 12mo, Cloth, $1 75.

BULWER'S KING ARTHUR. A Poem. By EARL LYTTON. New Edition. 12mo, Cloth, $1 75.

BURNS'S LIFE AND WORKS. The Life and Works of Robert Burns. Edited by ROBERT CHAMBERS. 4 vols., 12mo, Cloth, $6 00.

CARLYLE'S FREDERICK THE GREAT. History of Friedrich II., called Frederick the Great. By THOMAS CARLYLE. Portraits, Maps, Plans, &c. 6 vols., 12mo, Cloth, $12 00.

CARLYLE'S FRENCH REVOLUTION. History of the French Revolution. Newly Revised by the Author, with Index, &c. 2 vols., 12mo, Cloth, $3 50.

CARLYLE'S OLIVER CROMWELL. Letters and Speeches of Oliver Cromwell. With Elucidations and Connecting Narrative. 2 vols.,12mo,Cloth, $3 50.

CHALMERS'S POSTHUMOUS WORKS. The Posthumous Works of Dr. Chalmers. Edited by his Son-in-Law, Rev. WILLIAM HANNA, LL.D. Complete in 9 vols., 12mo, Cloth, $13 50.

DOOLITTLE'S CHINA. Social Life of the Chinese: with some Account of their Religious, Governmental, Educational, and Business Customs and Opinions. With special but not exclusive Reference to Fuhchau. By Rev. JUSTUS DOOLITTLE, Fourteen Years Member of the Fuhchau Mission of the American Board. Illustrated with more than 150 characteristic Engravings on Wood. 2 vols., 12mo, Cloth, $5 00.

GIBBON'S ROME. History of the Decline and Fall of the Roman Empire. By EDWARD GIBBON. With Notes by Rev. H. H. MILMAN and M. GUIZOT. A new Cheap Edition. To which is added a complete Index of the whole Work, and a Portrait of the Author. 6 vols., 12mo, Cloth, $9 00.

HARPER'S NEW CLASSICAL LIBRARY. Literal Translations.
The following Volumes are now ready. Portraits. 12mo, Cloth, $1 50 each.
CÆSAR.—VIRGIL.—SALLUST.—HORACE. — CICERO'S ORATIONS.—CICERO'S OFFICES, &c.—CICERO ON ORATORY AND ORATORS.—TACITUS (2 vols.).—TERENCE. — SOPHOCLES. — JUVENAL. — XENOPHON.— HOMER'S ILIAD.—HOMER'S ODYSSEY. — HERODOTUS.—DEMOSTHENES.—THUCYDIDES.—ÆSCHYLUS. —EURIPIDES (2 vols.).—LIVY (2 vols.).—PLATO.

EDGEWORTH'S (MISS) NOVELS. With Engravings. 10 vols., 12mo, Cloth, $15 00.

GROTE'S HISTORY OF GREECE. 12 vols., 12mo, Cloth, $18 00.

HELPS'S SPANISH CONQUEST. The Spanish Conquest in America, and its Relation to the History of Slavery and to the Government of Colonies. By ARTHUR HELPS. 4 vols., 12mo, Cloth, $6 00.

HALE'S (MRS.) WOMAN'S RECORD. Woman's Record; or, Biographical Sketches of all Distinguished Women, from the Creation to the Present Time. Arranged in Four Eras, with Selections from Female Writers of each Era. By Mrs. SARAH JOSEPHA HALE. Illustrated with more than 200 Portraits. 8vo, Cloth, $5 00.

HALL'S ARCTIC RESEARCHES. Arctic Researches and Life among the Esquimaux: being the Narrative of an Expedition in Search of Sir John Franklin, in the Years 1860, 1861, and 1862. By CHARLES FRANCIS HALL. With Maps and 100 Illustrations. The Illustrations are from Original Drawings by Charles Parsons, Henry L. Stephens, Solomon Eytinge, W. S. L. Jewett, and Granville Perkins, after Sketches by Captain Hall. 8vo, Cloth, $5 00.

HALLAM'S CONSTITUTIONAL HISTORY OF ENGLAND, from the Accession of Henry VII. to the Death of George II. 8vo, Cloth, $2 00.

HALLAM'S LITERATURE. Introduction to the Literature of Europe during the Fifteenth, Sixteenth, and Seventeenth Centuries. By HENRY HALLAM. 2 vols., 8vo, Cloth, $4 00.

HALLAM'S MIDDLE AGES. State of Europe during the Middle Ages. By HENRY HALLAM. 8vo, Cloth, $2 00.

HILDRETH'S HISTORY OF THE UNITED STATES. FIRST SERIES: From the First Settlement of the Country to the Adoption of the Federal Constitution. SECOND SERIES: From the Adoption of the Federal Constitution to the End of the Sixteenth Congress. 6 vols., 8vo, Cloth, $18 00.

HUME'S HISTORY OF ENGLAND. History of England, from the Invasion of Julius Cæsar to the Abdication of James II., 1688. By DAVID HUME. With the Author's Last Corrections and Improvements. To which is prefixed a short Account of his Life, written by himself. 6 vols., 12mo, Cloth, $9 00; Sheep, $11 40: Half Calf, $19 50.

JOHNSON'S COMPLETE WORKS. The Works of Samuel Johnson, LL.D. With an Essay on his Life and Genius, by ARTHUR MURPHY, Esq. Portrait of Johnson. 2 vols., 8vo, Cloth, $4 00.

KINGLAKE'S CRIMEAN WAR. The Invasion of the Crimea, and an Account of its Progress down to the Death of Lord Raglan. By ALEXANDER WILLIAM KINGLAKE. With Maps and Plans. Three Vols. ready. 12mo, Cloth, $2 00 per vol.

KINGSLEY'S WEST INDIES. The West Indies. At Last: A Christmas in the West Indies. By the Rev. CHARLES KINGSLEY. Illustrated. 12mo, Cloth, $1 50.

LAMB'S COMPLETE WORKS. The Works of Charles Lamb. Comprising his Letters, Poems, Essays of Elia, Essays upon Shakspeare, Hogarth, &c., and a Sketch of his Life, with the Final Memorials, by T. Noon Talfourd. Portrait. 2 vols., 12mo, Cloth, $3 00.

LIVINGSTONE'S SOUTH AFRICA. Missionary Travels and Researches in South Africa; including a Sketch of Sixteen Years' Residence in the Interior of Africa, and a Journey from the Cape of Good Hope to Loando on the West Coast; thence across the Continent, down the River Zambesi, to the Eastern Ocean. By David Livingstone, LL.D., D.C.L. With Portrait, Maps by Arrowsmith, and numerous Illustrations. 8vo, Cloth, $4 50.

LIVINGSTONE'S ZAMBESI. Narrative of an Expedition to the Zambesi and its Tributaries, and of the Discovery of the Lakes Shirwa and Nyassa, 1858-1864. By David and Charles Livingstone. With Map and Illustrations. 8vo, Cloth, $5 00.

DR. LIVINGSTONE'S LAST JOURNALS. The Last Journals of Dr. Livingstone in Central Africa, from 1865 to his Death. Continued by a Narrative of his Last Moments and Sufferings, obtained from his Faithful Servants Chuma and Susi. By Horace Waller, F.R.G.S., Rector of Twywell, Northampton. With Maps and Illustrations. 8vo, Cloth, $5 00. Cheap Edition, with Map and Illustrations, 8vo, Cloth, $2 50.

M'CLINTOCK & STRONG'S CYCLOPÆDIA. Cyclopædia of Biblical, Theological, and Ecclesiastical Literature. Prepared by the Rev. John M'Clintock, D.D., and James Strong, S.T.D. 5 vols. now ready. Royal 8vo. Price per vol., Cloth, $5 00; Sheep, $6 00; Half Morocco, $8 00.

RECLUS'S EARTH. The Earth: a Descriptive History of the Phenomena of the Life of the Globe. By Elisée Reclus. Translated by the late B. B. Woodward, and Edited by Henry Woodward. With 234 Maps and Illustrations, and 23 Page Maps printed in Colors. Second American Edition, with copious Index. 8vo, Cloth, $5 00.

RECLUS'S OCEAN. The Ocean, Atmosphere, and Life. Being the Second Series of a Descriptive History of the Life of the Globe. By Elisée Reclus. Translated. Illustrated with 250 Maps or Figures, and 27 Maps printed in Colors. 8vo, Cloth, $6 00.

SHAKSPEARE. The Dramatic Works of William Shakspeare, with the Corrections and Illustrations of Dr. Johnson, G. Steevens, and others. Revised by Isaac Reed. Engravings. 6 vols., Royal 12mo, Cloth, $9 00.

SMILES'S LIFE OF THE STEPHENSONS. The Life of George Stephenson, and of his Son, Robert Stephenson; comprising, also, a History of the Invention and Introduction of the Railway Locomotive. By Samuel Smiles. With Steel Portraits and numerous Illustrations. 8vo, Cloth, $3 00.

SMILES'S HISTORY OF THE HUGUENOTS. The Huguenots: their Settlements, Churches, and Industries in England and Ireland. By Samuel Smiles. With an Appendix relating to the Huguenots in America. Crown 8vo, Cloth, $1 75.

SMILES'S HUGUENOTS AFTER THE REVOCATION. The Huguenots in France after the Revocation of the Edict of Nantes; with a Visit to the Country of the Vaudois. By Samuel Smiles. Crown 8vo, Cloth, $2 00.

SPEKE'S AFRICA. Journal of the Discovery of the Source of the Nile. By Captain John Hanning Speke. With Maps and Portraits and numerous Illustrations, chiefly from Drawings by Captain Grant. 8vo, Cloth, uniform with Livingstone, Barth, Burton, &c., $4 00.

STRICKLAND'S (Miss) QUEENS OF SCOTLAND. Lives of the Queens of Scotland and English Princesses connected with the Regal Succession of Great Britain. By Agnes Strickland. 8 vols., 12mo, Cloth, $12 00.

THE STUDENT'S SERIES. 12mo, Cloth, $2 00 per vol.

France. Engravings.
Gibbon. Engravings.
Greece. Engravings.
Hume. Engravings.
Rome. By Liddell. Engravings.
Old Testament History. Engravings.
New Testament History. Engravings.
Strickland's Queens of England. Abridged. Engravings.
Ancient History of the East. Engravings.
Hallam's Middle Ages.
Hallam's Constitutional History of England.
Lyell's Elements of Geology. Engravings.

TENNYSON'S COMPLETE POEMS. The Complete Poems of Alfred Tennyson, Poet Laureate. With numerous Illustrations by Eminent Artists, and Three Characteristic Portraits. 8vo, Paper, 75 cents; Cloth, $1 25.

THOMSON'S LAND AND BOOK. The Land and the Book; or, Biblical Illustrations drawn from the Manners and Customs, the Scenes and the Scenery of the Holy Land. By W. M. Thomson, D.D., Twenty-five Years a Missionary of the A.B.C.F.M. in Syria and Palestine. With Two elaborate Maps of Palestine, an accurate Plan of Jerusalem, and *Several Hundred Engravings*, representing the Scenery Topography, and Productions of the Holy Land, and the Costumes, Manners, and Habits of the People. Two large 12mo Volumes, Cloth, $5 00.

TYERMAN'S WESLEY. The Life and Times of the Rev. John Wesley, M.A., Founder of the Methodists. By the Rev. Luke Tyerman, Author of "The Life of Rev. Samuel Wesley." Portraits. Three Vols. Crown 8vo, Cloth, $2 50 per vol.

TYERMAN'S OXFORD METHODISTS. The Oxford Methodists: Memoirs of the Rev. Messrs. Clayton, Ingham, Gambold, Hervey, and Broughton, with Biographical Notices of others. By Rev. Luke Tyerman. With Portraits. Crown 8vo, Cloth, $2 50.

TYSON'S ARCTIC EXPERIENCES. Arctic Experiences: containing Captain George E. Tyson's Drift on the Ice-Floe, a History of the Polaris Expedition, the Cruise of the Tigris, and Rescue of the Polaris Survivors. To which is added a General Arctic Chronology. Edited by E. Vale Blake. With Map and numerous Illustrations. 8vo, Cloth, $4 00.

RAWLINSON'S MANUAL OF ANCIENT HISTORY. A Manual of Ancient History, from the Earliest Times to the Fall of the Western Empire. Comprising the History of Chaldæa, Assyria, Media, Babylonia, Lydia, Phœnicia, Syria, Judæa, Egypt, Carthage, Persia, Greece, Macedonia, Parthia, and Rome. By George Rawlinson, M.A., Camden Professor of Ancient History in the University of Oxford. 12mo, Cloth, $2 50.

WOOD'S HOMES WITHOUT HANDS. Homes Without Hands: being a Description of the Habitations of Animals, classed according to their Principle of Construction. By J. G. Wood, M.A., F.L.S. With about 140 Illustrations. 8vo, Cloth, Beveled Edges, $4 50.

BELLOWS'S TRAVELS. The Old World in its New Face: Impressions of Europe in 1867, 1868. By Henry W. Bellows. 2 vols., 12mo, Cloth, $3 50.

HAZEN'S SCHOOL AND THE ARMY IN GERMANY AND FRANCE. The School and the Army in Germany and France, with a Diary of Siege Life at Versailles. By Brevet Major-General W. B. Hazen, U.S.A., Colonel Sixth Infantry. Crown 8vo, Cloth, $2 50.

COLERIDGE'S COMPLETE WORKS. The Complete Works of Samuel Taylor Coleridge. With an Introductory Essay upon his Philosophical and Theological Opinions. Edited by Professor Shedd. Complete in Seven Vols. With a fine Portrait. Small 8vo, Cloth, $10 50.

CPSIA information can be obtained
at www.ICGtesting.com
Printed in the USA
JSHW031055030322
23557JS00003B/9